"Can I help you?"

Andrea asked the most magnificent male she'd ever seen—and right here on her own front stoop.

She was quite taken aback by the look of out-and-out hostility she got in return. She shivered. What had she done to deserve that? Was he a new neighbor upset with the remodeling noise? If she promised to be very good, would he stop glaring at her?

What Greg saw was a little sprite, a woman who was a full foot shorter than his own height of six-two. She was swamped in an oversized man's shirt that had clearly served as a painting smock in the past. Snug jeans completed the ensemble, which—coupled with her wide-open baby-blue eyes—gave the effect of diminutive vulnerability.

Greg became even more irritated as he had to stamp down an urge to protect and covet. *Was this little shrew innocent? Vulnerable? No way!*

Dear Reader:

The spirit of the Silhouette Romance Homecoming Celebration lives on as each month we bring you six books by continuing stars!

And we have a galaxy of stars planned for 1988. In the coming months, we're publishing romances by many of your favorite authors such as Annette Broadrick, Sondra Stanford and Brittany Young. Beginning in January, Debbie Macomber has written a trilogy designed to cure any midwinter blues. And that's not all—during the summer, Diana Palmer presents her most engaging heros and heroines in a trilogy that will be sure to capture your heart.

Your response to these authors and other authors of Silhouette Romances has served as a touchstone for us, and we're pleased to bring you more books with Silhouette's distinctive medley of charm, wit and—above all—romance.

I hope you enjoy this book and the many stories to come. Come home to romance—for always!

Sincerely,

Tara Hughes
Senior Editor
Silhouette Books

TERRY ESSIG

House Calls

Silhouette Romance

Published by Silhouette Books New York

America's Publisher of Contemporary Romance

For Ellen Parent Caputo. She never
let me give up. Not for three long
years. Thanks, Ellen.

SILHOUETTE BOOKS
300 E. 42nd St., New York, N.Y. 10017

Copyright © 1988 by Terry Parent Essig

All rights reserved, including the right to reproduce
this book or portions thereof in any form whatsoever.
For information address Silhouette Books,
300 E. 42nd St., New York, N.Y. 10017

ISBN: 0-373-08552-4

First Silhouette Books printing January 1988

All the characters in this book are fictitious. Any
resemblance to actual persons, living or dead, is
purely coincidental.

SILHOUETTE, SILHOUETTE ROMANCE and colophon
are registered trademarks of the publisher.

America's Publisher of Contemporary Romance

Printed in the U.S.A.

TERRY ESSIG

says that her writing is her escape valve from a life that leaves very little time for recreation or hobbies. With a husband and five young children, Terry works on her stories a little at a time, between seeing to her children's piano, sax and trombone lessons, their gymnastics, ice-skating and swim team practices and her own activities of leading a Brownie troop, participating in a car pool and attending organic chemistry classes. Her ideas, she says, come from her imagination and her life—neither one of which is lacking!

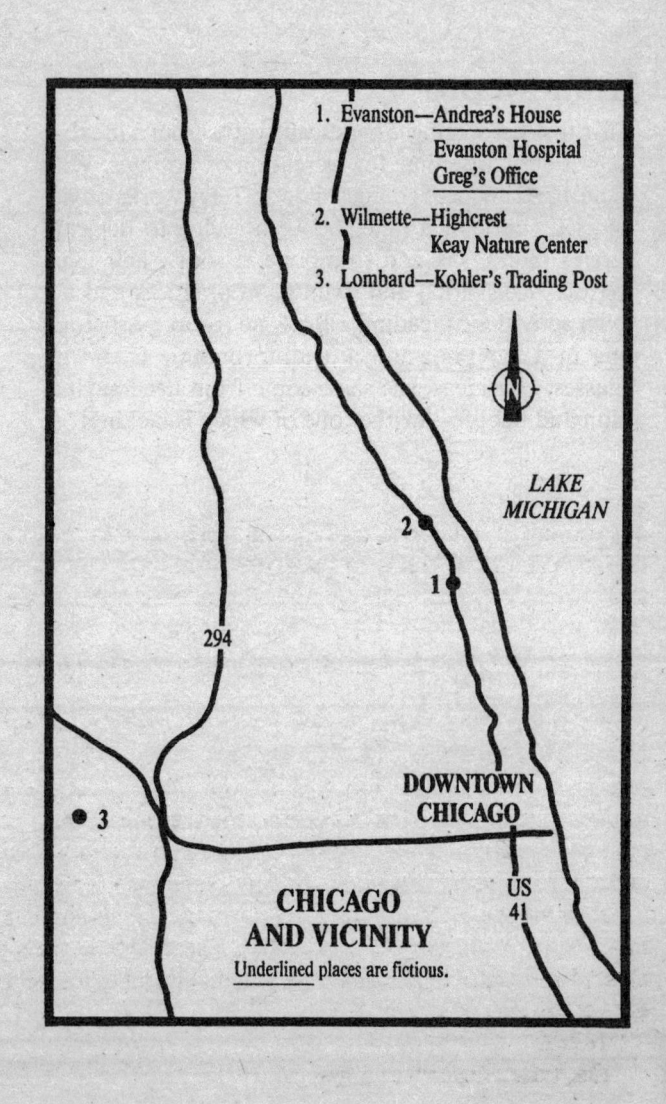

1. Evanston—<u>Andrea's House</u>
   Evanston Hospital
   <u>Greg's Office</u>
2. Wilmette—<u>Highcrest</u>
   <u>Keay Nature Center</u>
3. Lombard—<u>Kohler's Trading Post</u>

LAKE MICHIGAN

294

DOWNTOWN CHICAGO

US 41

CHICAGO AND VICINITY
<u>Underlined</u> places are fictious.

Chapter One

Returning the telephone to the phone company was one of the few things remaining to take care of before Greg Rennolds could leave the East Coast and long years of medical training behind forever. He was heading for the Midwest and a partnership in an ob-gyn practice in Chicago's northern suburb of Evanston.

The phone rang just as he was reaching for the plug. He jumped a good inch. "Lord," he muttered, "that just proves what bad shape I'm still in." He stared at it for a moment as its loud ring broke the silence once again. It couldn't be the hospital, he thought. His residency had ended two months ago. He had only come back to Baltimore to move his things after having spent the summer in Florida. It would be best to ignore it, he decided, telling himself it was probably just a wrong number. But in the next instant, his curiosity won out.

"Hello?"

"Oh, thank God I've caught you."

He should have ignored it. It was not an inconvenient wrong number. No, it was much more annoying than that; it was his sister Loretta. "Loretta, how are you? I was just on my way out the door. Long drive ahead of me, you know," he began heartily, hoping to head her off at the pass.

"And I'm so glad you haven't left yet, Greg. The most terrible thing has happened." Greg winced. His ploy had failed and his sister was off and running. His carefully planned time-table for the day had more than met its match. Sometimes he felt as if he were the elder sibling rather than the other way around. It was hard to believe Loretta was actually fifteen years his senior. She rarely acted it.

"Let me call you from Evanston. I want to get on the highway. Tomorrow afternoon, I promise."

"No, no. This won't take long." Famous last words, he thought, stifling a sigh and squatting on the floor. All his furniture had already been sold two months ago. Loretta rambled on, still skirting whatever point there was to her call. "You must take care of things the minute you hit the city limits."

"What city?"

Loretta sounded confused, which was nothing compared to what Greg felt. "Why, Evanston, of course. What else were we talking about?"

"Sorry, I'm still not operating up to par. What about Evanston's city limits?"

Loretta was silent for a moment. Greg would've bet she'd forgotten he'd just been released after a couple of weeks' enduring the wrong end of the hospitalization process. She must have felt guilty because she did pause long enough to inquire, "That's right, you haven't been well, have you?" He didn't need her to confirm it, he knew. "How are you feeling, dear?"

"Tired, too dragged out to go back to work. And yellow."

"Funny how hepatitis turns one yellow, isn't it?"

"'Funny' hardly describes it."

"You should never have donated your summer to that Cuban refugee camp."

Had he known he was going to stick himself with a needle he'd just used on a lady carrying the disease, he probably wouldn't have, he thought, looking at his watch. He really needed to get going. But Loretta evidently wasn't going to be swayed.

"Poor dear," she continued, evidently deciding that this was enough sympathy because she forged on, "But about Karen..."

Greg started getting that familiar ache over the bridge of his nose that Loretta seemed to bring on. "We were talking about Karen?" Karen was Loretta's only progeny and only a few years younger than Greg himself.

"Of course we were."

He sat back against the stained beige wall. He might as well get comfortable. "We talked about my being sick all summer in Florida and the fact that I'm getting a late start on a long drive halfway across the country to Illinois. When did we discuss Karen?"

His sister's tone was impatient. "You're moving to Evanston. Evanston, Illinois."

"Not if I don't get out of here and return the phone."

"And Karen is living in Evanston now."

"So?"

"I'd think you could show a little more concern for your niece's well-being, Gregory."

He thought about that for a moment. Karen's biggest problem was an independent streak a mile wide that usually put her in direct conflict with her overprotective mother. Other than that, she was as straight as an arrow. Maybe she was sick. Trust Loretta to call a doctor half a continent away. That must be it, he concluded.

But that wasn't it. "She's gone completely off the deep end. This pregnancy of hers has completely unglued her. I'm very worried, Greg."

Greg watched the shadows lengthening outside the apartment window. The phone store would be closing in an hour. "She and that boy she up and married have left that darling little apartment on Lee Street and moved in with a madwoman who has them slaving from dawn till dusk remodeling some hovel she calls a house."

It sounded rather like "Hansel and Gretel" to him. Only "that boy" was twenty-four years old and he couldn't see Karen as Gretel at all. She had a mind like a steel trap. Greg couldn't see her losing it over a few extra hormones.

"And you know how Karen insists on doing everything for herself. She won't discuss it with her father or me at all. You must go there first thing. Maybe she'll talk to you. The landlady probably needs to be taken to court. Whatever rent they pay, it's robbery. She must have some kind of hold on them. I just can't believe they haven't enough sense of their own to..."

Greg's headache was worsening by leaps and bounds. Right about now he'd promise his sister anything to get her off the phone. And he did.

The drive was even more grueling than he had anticipated. Coffee and cola only went so far in keeping him awake, and frequent rest stops were necessary. It was shortly after noon the following day when he finally pulled up in front of the address he had gotten from his sister as the scene of her concern. He turned off the engine, pulled his keys from the ignition, and stepped out of his car and into what seemed to him the twilight zone. He heard yelling and pounding and doors banging. With all the noise, the billowing puffs of white coming from the second-floor window could well have been the residue of cannon fire rather than the plaster dust he suspected it was.

Greg stood out on the curb, amazement showing in every line in his brow. Karen's voice was easy to identify. The only male rumbling had to be his niece's husband, Tim. That left two participating voices in the higher, feminine range to place.

The landlady had quite a rip-roaring scene going with these people. From the sound of it, Karen and Tim had their own battle going on as well. But even that didn't prevent the couple from horning in on the others by throwing in pithy observations when they deemed it necessary.

Reluctantly, disparaging this idea of his sister's every step of the way, Greg made his way to the front door, jumping as a piece of drywall sailed out the second-story window and into a dumpster parked below. Didn't everyone park dumpsters on their front lawn? Good heavens!

He began eavesdropping on the argument drifting down from the second floor and learned there was no working furnace in this Chicago bungalow. The landlady, addressed as Andrea, intended to warm the house with the living-room fireplace tonight when a cold front was predicted to come through. The voice of another woman they called Lisa argued with this Andrea person that she had to bite the bullet and get a new furnace. Andrea insisted throughout that they would all survive, just as the pioneers had.

Didn't the woman understand that pioneers had heated one-room cabins while she had an entire house with indoor plumbing and pipes that could burst? Greg knew Chicago. Ordinarily, Indian summer did not last into November, as it had this year. This lady's luck was running on overtime.

No one answered the doorbell's call, which gave Greg's ire a chance to rise another five notches. The third female voice, it became clear, was not a relative of Andrea's, but of Tim's. And when Tim refused to be drawn into their arguments concerning the furnace and his ability, or lack thereof, to do all the drywalling by himself, he ringingly advised his sister Lisa, to "Stop putting words in my mouth. I don't want Andrea changing her mind and throwing a woman five months pregnant out onto the streets. I can't support her yet. I'm only an *almost* lawyer, and *almost* only counts in horseshoes."

Greg saw red. And for probably the first time in his life, he decided that his sister's concerns were valid.

While he waited to see if a second doorbell ringing would break through the cacophony of sound inside, he was treated to a lecture from the heartless wench within telling Karen to "get away from all that plaster dust immediately." Not because it was bad for her in her condition but because "you're bothering Tim. Now go down to the kitchen and mix paint the way you're supposed to be doing."

Greg reached for the knocker, determined to make himself heard. He would remove Karen from this loony bin personally, with force if necessary. But before he could put action to thought, the door swung open, almost crowning him with the storm door. First one, then another female barreled through, slapping it wide with each passage.

"Lisa, I swear, if you call my family, I will never spea... Oh, hello." Andrea Conrades halted and turned. She had been so upset that she'd practically passed right by the most magnificent male form she had ever seen. And he was perched right here on her own front stoop. He had the kind of body a phys-ed teacher, such as herself, could really appreciate. Tall, with nicely shaped broad athletic shoulders, minimal hips and rear, just enough to fill out his tailored navy slacks to perfection. He had thick mahogany-colored hair with a riot of curls that cried out for a woman's fingers to instill a little order. Who might this interesting specimen be? she wondered. "Can I help you?" she questioned politely, all the while wondering if he already belonged to anybody. She was quite taken aback by the look of out-and-out hostility she got in return.

She shivered. What had she done to deserve that? Was he a new neighbor upset by the remodeling noise? If she promised to be very good would he stop glaring at her?

What Greg saw was a little sprite a full foot shorter than his own six foot two. She was swamped in an oversize men's shirt that clearly had served as a painting smock many times in the past. Snug jeans completed the ensemble, which, coupled with her wide-open baby-blue eyes, gave the effect of diminutive vulnerability.

Greg became even more irritated as he had to stamp down an urge to protect. But was this little shrew innocent? Vulnerable? No way! Disgruntled, he straightened to his full height advantage and informed her, "I'm here to see Mrs. Nyland." Somewhat sarcastically he added, "That is, if she can take a few minutes from painting and scrubbing without being tossed out onto the street."

Andrea's eyes widened at what she considered an unprovoked attack. "Who the heck are you?" she riposted. She tried not to let her size allow people to think she was a pushover, but whatever tactics she used seldom worked. The rude giant stalked past her as though she were of no consequence, and entered the small foyer.

"Screen her visitors, do you? Very wise," he said. "Otherwise, someone might slip her a file hidden in a cake and spring her out of this place." Impatiently he looked at the various paths he could take. "Which way? Through to the left or up the stairs?" Grudgingly, he tacked on, "I'm her uncle."

Andrea merely tapped her foot impatiently and placed arms akimbo, staring at him. "Her uncle, huh? Poor thing," she said. "Go to the left, she's back in my kitchen."

He pushed the left inside door open and strode into her living room. "Ah, yes. I do recall hearing you order her to paint the kitchen. In case you haven't noticed, she's pregnant. She shouldn't be breathing all those fumes or doing such strenuous work. It's your building, and you look perfectly capable of doing your own painting. The very picture of health, in fact."

Somehow, it didn't seem a compliment. He seemed irritated by her looks, and she didn't have to listen to insults in her own home. She trailed him into the living room. If he would just hold still long enough, she'd set him straight. "You don't have the foggiest idea—"

"As a doctor," he interrupted smugly, "I'm trained in differentiating the healthy from the un."

The pompous jerk.

Greg looked around at the simple but well-appointed room. The focal point was the fireplace at the far end with its beautiful marble trim. The stained-glass windows on either side were true to the characteristic layout of a Chicago bungalow.

In anticipation of the approaching solstice, the noontime sun already hung low in the southern sky, its streams of light bringing to jeweled life the violet blue iris and orange day-lily motif of the windows. The delicate tones were echoed throughout the room in the pastel patterned sofa, iris throw pillows and cream draperies with their bits of nubby orange and blue thread. The walls were also cream, the woodwork was stained to match the highly polished floors, and a shiny ebony baby-grand piano stood at one end of the room.

"Well, at least your apartment is quite nice," he commented before proceeding to the next room. He stopped and blinked at the empty kelly-green dining room, the walls of which hadn't even been spackled and primed. "I'll amend that. You have a nice front room. How much do you charge them to live in this dump, and is there anything in writing?"

The nerve of the man! "They've promised me their firstborn child," she responded sweetly.

"I heard them calling you Andrea. It's your last name that's Rumpelstiltskin, then?"

"No, it is not," she retorted spiritedly, not bothering to fill in the blank. "And for future reference, not that I expect there to be any need, the name is *Ann*drea, not Ahn*drea*. This is the Midwest, sonny. More specifically, this is Chicago. Your high-brow, patrician accent is wasted here."

"I'm sure it is, most particularly on you. Ahn*drea* is a far softer and more feminine pronunciation of the name," he pointed out, pushing his way through the half-stripped double French doors to the back of the house. "Just spare me the Chicagoese 'dese' and 'dose.' I'm not up for those at the moment."

She was getting tired of trailing him through her own home so she pushed in front of him to enter the kitchen first. "Karen," she said. "Your charming, silver-tongued, devil of an uncle has come to pay a call. You neglected to mention him, dear. Is he actually your uncle? He seems rather young for the role and much too obnoxious to be related to you."

Karen looked up from her labors at the ramshackle gray Formica table. "My gosh, I don't believe it!" She jumped up from her seat to hurtle herself across the room. "Greg! How are you? What are you doing here? Can you stay?"

Clearly the girl had no taste in relatives, Andrea thought. She sniffed. "I'm going out to see how Tim's coming with the wood chopping."

It was the wrong thing to say. The accusatory brown eyes of Karen's "uncle Greg" were back to their glaring.

"You do know you are required by law to maintain a certain temperature in a rental unit?" he started. "I believe it's sixty-five by day and fifty-five at night."

Andrea didn't bother to respond. Instead, she rolled her eyes meaningfully at Karen and said, "I can't handle any more today. Get rid of him, will you? Maybe he'll take you for a ride in that fancy car I saw parked out front."

When Karen and her uncle stood side by side, as they were now, she could see the family resemblance. Obviously the same trace of Italian ancestry flowed in their blood if the dark crop of tight curls each sported and the large, soulful brown eyes were anything to go by. Only Karen's complexion differed—much lighter and pinker than her uncle's creamed-coffee color.

Karen's delighted expression had drooped considerably at Andrea's request to dump Greg. Andrea sighed in resignation. "Never mind. I was going out anyway. It's probably not the wisest thing to do, but I'll leave you to him."

As she slammed out the back door she overheard Greg inquire, "Why is she bothering to paint in here? This room needs to be torched. Paint isn't even going to touch the problem."

Let Karen explain it to him. Andrea was trying so hard to organize her life. She was sick and tired of circumstances grabbing away the reins of control from her. Now here she was, virtually forced out of her own house. Who else would it happen to? She found Tim and told him that Greg was visiting. Then she stalked off on a vigorous neighborhood tour in an effort to cool down.

Even after the brisk walk, she wasn't quite up to facing the duo in the kitchen. She sat on a fat log waiting to be split and talked to Tim instead. "How come you're not in visiting with good old 'Uncle Greg'?"

"I thought I'd wait a bit for Karen to soothe his ruffled feathers." He leaned on the ax while shooting her a rueful glance from under thick blond brows. "I'm still feeling a bit raw about the situation myself. I'm not ready to have my face rubbed in it."

"You're doing the best you can, so don't be so hard on yourself. You tried family planning but nothing is infallible. It's not as though you weren't married when it came about. It's not your fault Karen had such bad morning sickness that she had to quit her job so early in the pregnancy."

"I should leave school and work full-time for a while. Finish up when the baby's a few years old. With just a part-time job, everything I earn has to go for books and tuition. It's not fair to dump my burden on you. I'm taking advantage of a friend."

"That's what a friend is for. This will work out fine, you'll see. You can't afford to pay rent without Karen's salary, and I can't afford to pay a contractor to remodel. Every penny I had went for the title to this place, such as it is. It would have taken me forever by myself. It's a perfect symbiotic relationship. You'll see. You'll feel differently when you've got your law degree in your back pocket this June."

"I suppose," he muttered gloomily. Reaching for the flannel shirt hanging gaily from a fence post, he slipped it across wide shoulders that strained against his snug white T-shirt. He didn't bother to button it or to tuck in the tail end. Extending a hand to Andrea, he pulled her from her perch. While she dusted her bottom with her free hand, he spoke with all the enthusiasm of a man facing imminent execution. "We might as well go in and face the music. If we're lucky, he'll have left."

"Sorry, but he seemed a bit determined to stick around. Tell me, how is it possible for her uncle to be so young? He's not much older than I am. Five, six years is all. He's thirty, at most."

Tim thought for a minute. "Karen explained it to me once. I think her mother was supposed to have been one of a kind, but Greg surprised them all fifteen years later as a change-of-life baby. Karen's mother turned forty-five last August as I recall, so I suppose Greg is right around thirty."

In an effort to spot the enemy Andrea stuck her head through the back door before going in. To her relief, the kitchen population had been reduced by one-half. "By George, I believe he's gone," she muttered in relief. Bravely now, she entered the room and spoke to Karen, who was bent over the open oven door.

"Your uncle's left, has he?" she questioned in self-satisfied tones. She ventured to the stove and held a match to the old-fashioned burner, deciding to make some tea. "Much as I love you, Karen, I have to say your uncle rather reconfirms my belief in the Darwinian theory of evolution. Definitely a direct link to our cave-living forebears: overbearing and underbrained." She continued conversationally, "How are the cookies coming? Did the paint fumes from the condensed milk and food coloring knock you out? Your uncle took a rather dim view of someone in your delicate condition painting, I can tell you."

Karen laughed. "You know good and well he thought you were coercing me into painting walls and woodwork, not butterfly-shaped cookies for a dry run of a Brownie troop project." She flipped the cookies expertly off the baking sheet and onto the limited countertop space to join the others already cooling.

"He never asked or gave me any opportunity to insert anything into his running monologue." She came over to view the product of Karen's labors. "How did they come out? Will it make a good project for them?"

"They're fine. I think the Brownies should be able to handle this all right. The only tricky part comes when you cut the dough circles in half and invert them to make the wings. Make sure the girls overlap them sufficiently onto the rectangular body pieces. They seem to have a tendency to break off otherwise. Painting the wings wasn't tricky at all. They'll like that part."

"Thanks. You're a sweetheart," Andrea complimented as she viewed the warm cookies. "These are really beautiful. I was worried the food coloring mixed with the condensed milk would turn brown as it baked, but these colors are still quite bright."

"Greg painted them while I cut them out."

"Your uncle? I wouldn't have thought he was the cookie-decorating type. More the 'me important doctor, you peon' sort."

"Umm. Well I think I should warn you that I put him to rest on your bed after he almost fell asleep in the cookie dough. I'm sure ninety percent of his being crabby was from exhaustion. He had a long drive here."

Andrea reached to absently brush flour from Karen's oversize shirt front. "My bed! What's wrong with a hotel? The Orrington isn't that far away. What's the matter with him, anyway? Why is he so tired?"

Karen tapped her spatula reflectively on the edge of the cookie sheet while turning off the flame under the whistling teakettle with the other hand. "I'm not actually sure.

I was too busy trying to convince him you weren't an ogre to find out. But I will," she stated positively.

Andrea believed her. Karen never yelled, threw things or had tantrums. She was very low-key. Somehow, though, she always ended up with precisely what she had set out to achieve. Karen never lost control of the situation the way she herself did.

"Did you convince him?"

"What?" The other girl looked puzzled.

"That I'm not an ogre," she clarified.

"Oh, well, I sowed the seeds of doubt. Now it's up to you."

Andrea snorted her opinion of that suggestion in an unladylike fashion. "He won't be around long enough to make it worth my while." Too bad, too. What a body on that man! After pouring the steaming water into the pot, she threw in the teabags that Karen had set on the countertop for her. "Why is he in my bed? What's wrong with yours?"

"You know perfectly well as soon as Tim is done stacking logs on the porch, he's going to come in and insist I lie down for a while." Karen's eyes rolled skyward. "As though cookie baking is enough to physically exhaust me."

"Pregnant women need rest," Andrea stated empirically, gathering up a stack of cookies to have with their tea.

"I don't stand a chance against the two of you. But," Karen threatened with a jabbing forefinger, "I'm going to ask my doctor at my next appointment exactly how much sleep I need. Then look out!" She grabbed three cups and plopped down on the old stainless-steel kitchen chair.

Her husband entered to wash his hands at the sink. "Did you get a chance to nap yet, Karen?"

"Oh, yes," she lied sweetly to his back. "A good forty-five minutes at least."

"I haven't been gone forty-five minutes," he pointed out while Andrea laughed at Karen's caught with-a-hand-in-the-cookie-jar expression. "As soon as you're done with your tea, go in and lie down. You're just now getting over that awful morning sickness, and I don't want it to come back."

"Yes, master," his spouse grumbled.

"And don't you forget it," he ordered, kissing the top of her head.

"I'm fine now, you know. Have been for two weeks. I just wish you'd both believe that. Maybe you should come talk to the doctor with me."

"Why? What do you want to know?"

All heads turned to the drooping male propped against the kitchen doorframe. He shrugged his shoulders at their questioning looks and padded shoeless into the kitchen, grabbing a cup on his way to the table. "I couldn't sleep with all the racket," he explained, as though his tiredness was all their fault. "I hope whatever that is has some caffeine in it. I'll need it if I'm to spend the afternoon apartment hunting. I had planned to take care of finding a place a few weeks ago, but I was too out of it to do it."

Why did she feel like apologizing for making noise in her own home, Andrea wondered. But she knew. For all his tiredness, this was a man used to taking charge. Wherever he stood, it became his turf. He exuded confidence and control, even when dead on his feet, and that charismatic aura was making her feel a trespasser in her own kitchen.

"Why are you so tired? What's wrong with you? You look in terrific physical shape, you should have plenty of energy." She sprawled back in her chair, letting her arms dangle as she studied him. "And why are you apartment hunting up here? If you're such a hotshot doctor, don't you have a medical practice somewhere?"

He returned her perusal while she poured the tea. They both ignored Karen wrangling with her spouse over her impending nap. "I am apartment hunting because I have just finished my specialization and passed my boards. I am now certified in ob-gyn as well as internal medicine and pharmacology. I bought into a practice here in Evanston. I was supposed to start six weeks ago, but I've had a run-in with a hepatitis B carrier. See how yellow the whites of my eyes are?" He leaned forward to give her a closer look.

She retreated.

At her reluctant nod, he continued, "I'm over the infectious part, but I'm still left with this jaundice and rotten sense of pervading fatigue, both of which should clear up in the next few weeks. I think I must have been rather rundown from the stress of years of medical training. It shouldn't be taking this long to get my strength back." He stopped talking to take a sip of tea, but the cup never reached his mouth. He stared into its confines instead.

"It's only tea, it won't hurt you." Even if she did make it on the weak side, surely his look of utter repugnance was overreaction.

"Uh, Andrea?" Tim too was studying his cup.

"Yes, Tim?"

"Is this some new kind of herbal tea we're trying?"

"No. Why do you ask?" She sat up straight in her chair to take a closer look in her cup. "My goodness. The tea is blue!" She looked up incredulously, trying to figure out what had happened to her normally brown brand. This brew wasn't even the light tan she generally achieved from her chintzy habit of using only one bag per pot. It was a biliously brilliant azure.

"Where'd you get the teabags?" Karen asked.

"It was sitting out on the counter. Didn't you put them out for me?" She blinked again at the oddly colored concoction.

"That explains it, then."

"It does?"

"Sure." Karen waved her hand in easy dismissal. "I had set them out to make a cup of tea while Greg and I talked, but I spilled some of the blue food dye there. I meant to throw them out, but I must have forgotten."

Andrea was tipping her cup in all directions, fascinated with the blue-tinted contents. "If you say so. Too bad it isn't Easter. This would make a wonderful color bath for eggs."

Tim rose to collect the cups and dump them into the sink. "Be that as it may, at the moment I have to go to work." He pointed at his wife. "You have to rest, and you two can start over with fresh bags."

"No, thanks." Greg rose slowly, noticing Andrea's orange-stained lips and Karen's green ones—proof of the painted cookies potency. The woman was probably harmless enough, as Karen insisted, but still crazy. He ought to get out while he could, his sister be hanged. "I think I've lost my yen for tea." He would like to talk to Karen, however. Looking at Tim, he asked, "Is it all right for Karen to come apartment hunting with me? We could do some visiting and she knows the neighborhoods where I should look. I won't let her overdo."

Tim looked doubtful, but at Karen's eager expression, relented. "Well, okay. Being a doctor, you should be able to tell if she looks strained."

Karen gave her husband a hug and a peck of a kiss. "Thanks. We'll be back for dinner so you won't have to eat alone, Andrea."

"Don't worry about me. It's an easy out for my turn at cooking," she said.

"Oh, no, you don't. We'll be here. You'll eat something awful if we don't show up," Karen insisted.

Greg let loose an exasperated growl. "I've never seen such an overprotective crew. Don't any of you believe in live and let live?"

"Andrea doesn't think it's worthwhile to cook for only one. You should see some of the stuff she came up with before we started eating together," Karen informed her uncle.

"So it's up to us to save her from herself, huh?"

The peace of an empty house was a soothing balm to Andrea's thoroughly irritated frame of mind. She seared a pot roast on both sides, threw in chunks of viciously chopped vegetables along with a can of cream of mushroom soup, and clunked the heavy cast-iron lid on the pot to let it simmer for the next three hours. The rest of the afternoon was spent chiseling nauseating pink-and-gray-swirled plastic tiles from the bathroom walls and muttering a great deal as she continually scraped her knuckles in the process.

Dinnertime came, marked only by a phone call reporting that Karen and Greg would eat out after all so they could keep looking for an apartment. Andrea warned them of Tim's ire, but they seemed unimpressed. She turned off the pot roast, ate an apple and a wedge of cheddar cheese instead and went back to the bathroom muttering.

The predicted cold front arrived. The temperature on the thermometer was dropping as though it had developed a leak. Hopefully the heat exchanger she had bought for the fireplace would live up to the claims of its flamboyant brochure. The fire was no problem for a former Girl Scout, and it was soon crackling cheerfully. After flicking the hearth insert's motor on, she left to ease her body into and out of a hot tub. She was snugly encased in a floor-length crimson velour robe, contentedly reading and toasting her toes in front of the roaring blaze when the various troops returned.

Karen plunked dispiritedly on the sofa, pulling Greg down beside her. "I never realized how many tacky apartments there were in this town."

"Yeah. The only decent one we saw isn't available for subleasing for another month," Greg moaned in return. "I guess I'll have to take a room at the Orrington. I hate living out of a suitcase in a hotel room."

"You'll find something tomorrow," Andrea muttered encouragingly, knowing in her heart what was going to happen but refusing to face it. She watched as Greg lay his head back on the sofa to close his eyes disconsolately. The man was exhausted.

Tim, who had just wandered in from stocking grocery shelves at the Dominick's market, noticed it too. "You're too tired to go to a hotel tonight," Tim stated. "This sofa opens into a bed. Karen and I will sleep here, and you take ours."

Greg looked up. "What? Oh, no, it's all right. Don't worry about me." He smiled bravely and hoped they'd go for it. He wasn't about to stay in this loony bin even one night. Blue tea and painted cookies. Good Lord, he thought, what next?

Andrea sighed. Here it was again. Another stray washing up on her doorstep, and she was powerless to prevent it. She had led a relatively blameless life. Why did the gods continually torment her like this?

"The pull-out sofa is too small for Karen and her stomach, let alone the two of you. I'll stay here and feed the fire. Greg can sleep in my bed," she said resignedly.

There was no contradictory argument coming from the dark form slumped against the sofa back. When she looked closer, his even breathing told the story: he had drifted to sleep in the middle of the discussion. Waifism must run in Karen's family. "Karen, turn down the bed. Tim, help me get him in there. I'll get his suitcase from the car while you undress him."

By the time she struggled in with the suitcase, Tim had him under the blankets with barely a murmur of acknowledgement. Andrea's rummaging through his bag didn't reveal any pajamas, so she pulled a man's robe from the case and lay it across the bottom of the bed before closing the door behind her.

Throwing two more logs on the fire, she made herself as comfortable as possible on a bed that spent most of its time folded into thirds. With concentrated effort, she was soon asleep herself. Vague forms of dark-skinned, broad-shouldered men with tousled mahogany hair and bodies that Michelangelo could have chiseled flitted through her dreams. They smiled and beckoned her near only to freeze her out with accusing, icy stares when she drew close. She didn't feel particularly well rested when morning finally arrived. She blamed it on the permanent creases in the sofa-bed mattress, along with the necessity of rising twice during the night to toss more wood onto the fire.

Chapter Two

Andrea found a pale primrose thermal running suit neatly folded by the washing machine. Thank goodness she wasn't too efficient about putting clean clothes away immediately, as she had no idea when access to her room might be regained.

Force of long-standing habit got her up at six in the morning. Since company was hard to come by at that hour, Andrea generally breakfasted alone. She crept into the kitchen in her socks and reached on tiptoe for the blender. Then she mixed her breakfast. Someday she would get around to rearranging the cabinets. The glasses were up much too high for a person her height. The tumbler she managed to flick to the edge of the high shelf seemed to have a life of its own. It teetered precariously for a moment. Then, as her usually quick reactions failed her, it slipped over the edge and shattered. She stood there in her socks, not wanting to move for fear of picking up a shard the hard way—with her foot. As she debated the alternatives, her bedroom door opened and a rumpled head of hair appeared.

"What's going on?"

"Don't come out here without shoes," she warned. "I've just dropped a glass, and there are slivers all over the floor."

"Right. Don't move. I'll be there in a second." He disappeared, but only momentarily. When he came back, he was in the thick green terry robe Andrea had left on the bed for him. But that, paired with yesterday's perfectly polished wing tips made him look ridiculous.

As Greg picked her up and set her on the edge of the cabinet top, he noticed the way she was avoiding his eyes. Correctly surmising the cause, he threatened, "Laugh, and I'll leave you stranded there." He made a disgusted sound as he studied her averted face and dancing eyes. "Never mind. Where's the broom?"

She pointed and then watched as he efficiently disposed of the broken pieces. As he lifted her down once more to the floor, she asked, "Are you going back to bed or would you like some breakfast? There's enough here for two."

"I might as well stay up. I used to be quite an early riser."

"Until six weeks ago?"

"You've got it. It's all I can do to drag myself out of bed at all lately." He looked around at the empty range top. "Exactly what is it there's enough for two of?"

Andrea indicated the blender. "If you could just get down two glasses..."

"That's all you're having? A glass of juice?"

"It has everything you could possibly need," she primly informed him.

He snorted his opinion of that. "That shows how much you know about nutrition." He studied the odd-looking concoction. "This is damn peculiar-looking orange juice."

"Just drink it. It'll make hair grow on your chest."

"I already have hair on my chest, and you sure as hell don't need any." He questioned suspiciously, "You're a health-food nut, aren't you? What's in here?"

"Oh, a little of this and a little of that."

"How very scientific. Could you possibly be a little more specific?" He set the glass she had handed him back on the countertop. "On second thought, never mind. I don't think I want to know. I don't suppose I could talk you into some bacon and eggs?" He offered the suggestion hopefully. "I'll replace them for you as soon as the stores open."

"No point in getting a lot of pans dirty for just the two of us. Besides, bacon is bad for you—high in cholesterol and all of that—and there are eggs right in here." She handed his glass right back to him.

He was turning a little green. "This is a liquid. It would logically follow that any eggs in here would have to be raw." He hadn't gotten an A in logic for nothing.

"Umm," she agreed.

"What else?" he whispered hoarsely.

"Fresh banana, six ounces of concentrated orange juice, milk, wheat germ, lecithin and a little brewer's yeast." She drained her glass. "Drink up, it's good for you."

"Oh, no. You *are* a health-food nut. I have to get out of here while I'm still quasi-normal."

She tried not to laugh. She really did. Clearly he viewed sanity as some tangible commodity over which he maintained only tenuous control. "You can't waste it. At least give it a try."

"I can't believe I'm really doing this," he muttered before taking a tentative swallow of the loathsome mixture. She was surprised he didn't hold his nose. "This will probably raise my voice an octave."

"Be truthful, now," she warned while watching closely for his reaction. "And remember, Adele Davis will come and get you in the still of the night if you say anything too nasty about her recipes."

"You mean this stuff actually came out of a recipe book?" She noted the amazement in his voice. "Actually, it's not that bad. Drinkable. I'd still prefer bacon and eggs, though," he qualified, finishing the contents of the glass in one brave gesture before setting it down with a thump.

He watched in growing consternation when, after giving a warm giggle, Andrea began to search for something—first looking under the table, then behind the kitchen door, and finally in the bathroom.

Eyeing her cautiously, he asked, "Uh, is there anything wrong?"

"Hmm? Oh, I can't remember where I left my running shoes. I don't want to wake Tim and Karen with my banging about, so I thought I'd go jogging. By the time I get back, they should be up, and I can start working around here."

"Ah, I can help with that. They're right by your bed. Banged my shin when I tripped over them to come investigate the racket out here. Be right back."

He disappeared into the bedroom while Andrea rinsed out the blender.

"Can I come with you?" he questioned as he produced the shoes.

She looked shocked. "I wouldn't think a man who keeps falling asleep at the drop of a hat would be a very likely candidate for a five-mile run."

"That far, huh?" He seemed genuinely disappointed. "I was hoping to start building back up. I used to do ten miles, but I expect I shouldn't try more than two or three to start now."

From what she had seen, he shouldn't try more than a brisk walk around the block. On the other hand as she eyed his physique in an appraising manner, Andrea was forced to admit, "With a body like that, I can well believe you used to be fairly physically active." Even an untrained eye would have to admire his perfect form, she thought before doing a double take. Her candid remark had disconcerted him to the point where he was actually blushing. His reentry into the real world after years of concentrated academia was going to hit him hard.

"Tell you what," she offered magnanimously. "We'll go to a track I know of nearby. Then we can both do what we want without leaving the other behind. You get dressed while I find my keys."

Greg was quick, and they left the house, closing the door quietly behind them. As they drove to the track, Andrea noticed that the weather was crisp and clear, perfect for running. Soon Andrea was well into her third mile, but it was not going well. She was so interested in keeping an eye on Greg who, even recovering from a serious illness, was such a supple study in lithe symmetry as he alternated running and walking around the track, that she stumbled and ignominiously skidded on her stomach several feet along the gravelly path. It seemed Greg was instantly at her side, helping her up and checking with a practiced hand for injuries.

"Here, let me see."

Andrea, who had been peering down the neck of her sweatshirt to check for damage, snapped the yellow top back against her chest. "Fat chance."

He took her hands firmly in his and pulled her over to the car, opening the door and sitting her sideways on the seat. "Don't be childish. I'm a doctor, remember? I doubt your stomach is anything special.

Stomach? She had thought he'd wanted to check... Suddenly, her thoughts were cut short. For someone who had recently been so sick, he was amazingly strong. By now he had both her hands effortlessly under control in one of his and was reaching for her sweat top with the other. She wriggled uselessly.

"Hold still," he commanded.

"Greg," she said, looking him directly in the eye. "I'm telling you I'm fine. I don't want you to do this, okay?"

He stopped and searched her face for a long moment. Slowly, he nodded his head and released her. "Okay. Not if you're not willing. But you're passing up a golden opportunity to have the damages checked by an expert. And there would have been no charge for a good looker like you." He leered and winked uncharacteristically as he stepped back.

Andrea relaxed and figured she had it made when he continued, back in his doctor role, "You don't seem to be wearing a bra, though. A woman's breasts need to be supported during exercise, you know. Otherwise you can tear the underlying supporting muscles."

Even though—as a physical education teacher—she knew he was right, she refused to discuss underwear with him or even look at him, studying instead the padded gray vinyl of the car's interior roofing. Not everyone practiced what they preached all the time.

"And how long has it been since your last checkup?" he badgered, on a favorite soapbox now. "You women let these things ride far too—"

"Six months. It's only been six months. Come back and yell at me some time next spring, all right?"

Greg was in the driver's seat now, reaching to switch on the ignition of his car. Andrea never had found her keys. He seemed determined to get in the last word. "At least get a good sports bra. Liberated women sag, especially liberated athletic women."

"I haven't got anything to sag," she informed him through gritted teeth, her face going red in spite of herself.

"I'm sure you have as much as ninety percent of the women I see. Women seem to be hypersensitive about breast size for some reason."

Andrea thought about the women Greg had seen and the one he had almost seen a moment ago. A warm flush crept over her, and she was very much afraid that Greg would not attribute her rise in color to her jogging. She leaned back against the navy fabric seat and directed all her mental powers to calming herself.

Noontime found Greg and Tim sitting at the kitchen table watching Andrea set a large cast-iron pot on top of the stove. She placed metal trivets inside and poured in a few inches of boiling water. Then she mixed cornmeal, whole-wheat and white flours, molasses, eggs, baking powder and raisins into a sticky mass and poured it all into two old metal cans she had washed and saved. Covering their tops with tinfoil, she carefully lowered them onto the trivets and adjusted the flame under the steaming bath.

"I'd ask her what she was doing," Greg remarked to no one in particular, "but after the breakfast she made, I'm afraid to find out."

Tim ignored him, instead fixing Andrea with a baleful glare. "I can't believe you're doing this to me. You know the smell of that stuff permeates the entire house, and it takes three damn hours for it to cook!"

"I knew it would be something awful," Greg moaned fatalistically.

Andrea was feeling decidedly picked on. "There was nothing wrong with that breakfast other than the fact your taste buds are all in your toes," she snapped in exasperation before turning on Tim in wounded tones. "I thought you liked this."

Apparently feeling rather persecuted himself, Tim reproached her, "You're going to tantalize me for the next three hours with the perfume of home-baked Boston brown bread..."

Greg perked up at that.

"And then you're going to tell me it's for somebody at work who needs a boost. I know you," Tim finished.

Greg sank back down in the chair with a disappointed air, his posture again echoing Tim's.

Andrea gave him a look of haughty disdain before yelling into the other room, "Karen! The pot roast I made for you ingrates for dinner last night is just about heated. Come on."

"Sure." Tim sniffed, his martyrdom evident. "We get reheated pot roast while some perfect stranger gets my Boston brown bread."

She took great pleasure in informing him, "It's for someone strange all right. You! It's a treat you'll get after you finish sealing the drywall in the upstairs apartment this afternoon."

"It is?" His posture straightened miraculously.

"A little bit of incentive. The sooner you two are up there living and out of my hair, the better I'll like it."

Tim got up and swung her into a Valentino-like dip. Then he kissed her soundly, right in front of his wife. "You'll miss us when we're gone, you sweet thing," he predicted, cheerfully beginning to toss the plates with the atrociously gaudy pink and lavender floral design onto the table. Sniffing the air appreciatively as he passed the stove on his way to the silverware drawer, he rubbed his hands together and gleefully intoned, "It's mine, all mine. Look out, drywall, here I come."

"I don't suppose you'd consider sharing a piece with a poor sick relative who needs his strength built back up?"

"No way, buddy." Then Tim appeared to reconsider. "Unless, of course, you want to help me seal the walls so we can get to it sooner."

"Do you have cream cheese to go with it?" Greg questioned Andrea. Then at her nod he agreed, "Right. I'll do it."

Andrea was stunned. "What about your apartment hunting?" If Greg spent his limited energy reserves helping Tim, she'd never get rid of him. This was her home, not a motel, yet the guests seemed to keep multiplying.

"You and Karen go," Greg suggested offhandedly. "The realtor knows my price range and specifications, and Karen knows my taste. It might be fun for you, but I'm finding it draining."

"Painting isn't draining? Besides, Karen needs to nap."

"Karen is as healthy as a horse." The recipient of that observation didn't look quite sure whether she should be pleased by that or not. "You two are killing her with kindness. She'll have a much easier delivery if she's in shape."

Andrea was doubtful of that, but agreed because her only option was helping Tim herself, and she hated sealing drywall. The sealant always dripped in her face and down her legs and arms. She said nothing further.

The roast and accompanying vegetables were piled on a platter and placed in the center of the rickety table along with a bowl of apple sauce and a basket of biscuits. Tim played head of the house, carving the meat into servable pieces. He directed his remarks to Andrea. "So, chief, what do we do about the furnace? The heat-exchange unit in the fireplace is working fine while the temperatures are above freezing, but we both know it's all downhill from here in the temperature department for at least three months." He took the platter back after Karen had served herself and spooned extra carrots onto her plate. "Eat those," he ordered.

Rolling her eyes skyward, Karen groaned, "I certainly hope you can learn to love Rubenesque women because that's what you're going to be left with when this is all over." He refused to be stared down, and she finally gave in, albeit ungraciously. "Okay, I'll eat them, but you'll be sorry."

"I'll take my chances," he said in a no-nonsense voice. "You lost too much weight with all that morning sickness."

"It isn't necessary to make it all up in one sitting."

He ignored her and turned expectantly to Andrea. "Well?"

Andrea sighed in reply. "I should have some money by the end of next week. It's the beginning of a new term for all my exercise classes. It was supposed to be a start on remodeling the kitchen, but it'll cover the cost of a new furnace." She gave a delicately rueful shrug. "I guess we can live with this excuse of a kitchen for a while longer."

Greg's dark eyes were intently studying her. "So you do plan to replace the furnace?"

Her puzzled eyes met his. "Of course. What did you expect?"

"I must say that's a relief. For a while there, I thought you had something against central heating. On a back-to-nature kick or some such thing. Why didn't you want Tim's sister to call your family for help?"

"Oh, my." Andrea cringed at the mere thought. "If they ever found out how bad this place was, they'd descend like the plague. The whole place would be redone in twenty-four hours or less—all very livable and all very tacky. None of it would be me. I'd rather do it myself, my own way, and wait until I can afford to buy what I want and not buy just to buy."

"I can understand that." He nodded in agreement. "My parents couldn't understand why I had to go into debt and go to Johns Hopkins for medical school. But I wanted the best education I could get." Suddenly disconcerted to find himself agreeing with her on an issue, he made an obvious move to change topics. He cut another bite of tender roast and had the forkful almost to his mouth before complimenting her. "This is really good...especially after eight years of hospital-cafeteria food. Is it hard to make? I'd like to learn to cook now that I'll have more time." His mouth was open, ready to accept the morsel coated in its rich brown broth.

"It's quite easy. Adding a can of cream of mushroom soup at the beginning is the whole trick. As the roast simmers, it makes a delicious gravy."

His mouth snapped shut. "You made the gravy with soup?"

"As long as it tastes good, who cares? You couldn't tell it wasn't scratch gravy." She shrugged. "Same with the biscuits. If you can't tell the difference, why bother?"

"Oh God. What's wrong with the biscuits?"

"Nothing. But they're not scratch either. I made them from a mix. I only care about the end product, not how I get there," she defended. "Cream of mushroom soup makes a terrific gravy. Better than I could do on my own, that's for sure."

Greg's head shot up, and he looked as if he were about to gag. "Mushrooms? Did you say mushroom soup? I hate mushrooms!"

Three sets of eyes swung to his plate; its pink and purple flowers previously covered with healthy servings of meat and vegetables were once again visible. He'd made short work of a large amount of food that he claimed to dislike.

"Did you bother to inform your stomach of that fact?" Andrea inquired with acid sweetness. "You certainly looked as though you were enjoying it, mushrooms notwithstanding." Here was a classic example of an intelligent, well-educated man allowing childish prejudices to ruin an adult enjoyment of good food.

His attention turned to his openmouthed niece. "Why didn't you warn me she went in for poisoning her victims?"

"Hey," Karen protested. "She's taught me everything I know about cooking. I think it's terrific. You were enjoying it yourself until someone mentioned mushrooms and soup. It must be the hepatitis that's made you so intolerant and crabby. You never used to be like this."

"Living in this house has changed you. Your mother was right to worry," he informed her darkly before turning to Tim. "Get out while you can. You two would be better off on welfare. First thing you know she'll have the baby hooked on canned soups instead of formula."

"Right, that tears it." Andrea threw her napkin on her plate, glaring at Greg who was cautiously tasting a small amount of the potato he had been hungrily downing moments before.

"They must not use a whole lot of mushrooms in the soup," he judiciously decided. "You really can't taste them."

Andrea rose disgustedly from the table, pulling Karen with her. To think she had actually been softening toward him! "Where and at what time are we supposed to meet this realtor?" She would move the heavens if necessary to find the turkey an apartment—one available immediately.

After receiving the necessary data, she grabbed her car keys from the kitchen windowsill and spitefully directed Tim, "I don't care how much he paints. He only gets one slice of bread, do you hear me?"

Tim saluted, "I hear and obey, O mistress of the house." Then he directed Greg, "Since I know where the supplies are, I'll get things lined up while you take my turn at the dishes."

But Tim's glee at escaping the sudsy water was quickly dashed by his earnest wife. "That's not fair," she interjected. "We'll just put him in the rotation, and you can delay your turn until dinner."

Her uncle's next remark illustrated how adulthood could serve to strip the rosy glow from a bad case of hero worship. "Dishes are women's work!" Greg protested, which caused Karen's mouth to gape in shock. "Tim, you've been brainwashed," he added. Then, seeing all three implacable expressions, he turned dejectedly to the pile by the sink. "Okay, I'll do them. You two just find me an apartment I can move into tonight, understand?"

Andrea was determined to do her best.

Five-and-a-half long hours later, Andrea pulled herself once more from the cramped confines of her little yellow car. She glanced absently at the sky as she and Karen trudged through the bungalow's backyard and reflected on the seasons. November was traditionally the most overcast month of the year in Chicago. This November appeared to be trying to outdo itself. The thick gray blanket hanging ominously overhead accurately reflected Andrea's bleak mood. Karen had found some insignificant flaw in each of the apartments they'd seen. Frankly, Andrea thought she had been nitpicking. But why? Surely she could sense the antipathy between Andrea and her uncle. And even Karen must be feeling the space crunch. Well, good old Uncle Greg could go to the hotel tonight and carry on his search himself. Tomorrow was Monday, and Andrea had to go back to work.

Her heart sank at the sight greeting their return. Tim and Greg were descending from the second story, painting supplies in hand. Spatters of white paint added to their pallor and general air of fatigue. Tim was dragging, but Greg had been absolutely done in. Andrea suspected that sheer contrariness was all that kept him still moving.

"I think I may have overdone it a bit today," he admitted. "All those weeks of forced inactivity have every muscle in my body aching from today's light workout. I can't see how I'm going to be able to put in full days at the medical center in just a week's time," he added disconsolately.

Clearly it would take a heartless shrew to send a man in his state of exhaustion to an impersonal hotel. The big baby, he would undoubtedly recover more quickly during the next few days with the placebo of Karen's hovering love and concern. Then he would have to go, Andrea decided. Positively by the end of the week. Karen and Tim would be occupying the upper apartment by then, and she wanted the first floor to herself again after two months of communal living.

She carried the brown grocery bag into the kitchen and emptied the supplies onto the countertop. "I'll make dinner while you two get cleaned up. The tile grouting in the upstairs bathroom has had over twenty-four hours to dry. Why don't you shower up there, Tim? Greg can soak his sore muscles in a hot tub down here."

She could hear the upstairs shower as she ushered her unwilling victim toward the steaming bath she had prepared. "Stop treating me like an invalid," he protested. "I'm just a little tired." As Andrea closed the door on his complaints, he raised his voice again. "I noticed this morning there's no lock on this door. If you want me to get in here, you'll have to keep everyone away. I'm not into exhibitionism."

"Not to worry," she called sweetly as she went to drag out the brandy bottle. Where had she stuck the brandy snifters? After giving him enough time to have taken off his clothes and gotten into the tub, she knocked on the bathroom door. Andrea could hear the water swish as Greg sat up suddenly. She could imagine the panic on his virile but inhibited features as he called in a slightly panicked voice.

"Yes?"

"I thought a little brandy might help you relax," she called through the door, having a hard time not giggling. The way he answered, she knew his teeth were clenched.

"No, thank you."

"Oh, well, want me to see if I can knead out some of the knots in your back?" She jiggled the doorknob and wondered if Italians ever went completely pale. It might be a genetic impossibility.

He was a lot of fun to tease right now, but even in his present condition there was a blatant masculine virility about him that told her getting the best of him was a crime she wouldn't get away with in more normal times. She was living dangerously, but some inner devil made her press on. Andrea pushed the door open a crack, just enough to see the bare beginnings of the bathroom's old-fashioned white octagonal floor tiles. Water splashed again. He must be reaching for something to cover himself with.

"Don't you dare come in here," Greg warned.

"Just relax. I seriously doubt you have anything I haven't seen before." That was true enough. Her college roommate had kept a hunk-of-the-month poster pinned to their dorm room bulletin board. She joked that it was to remind her why she was in school.

"I hope you're enjoying this," he called in dangerously soft tones, "because you're going to pay."

Andrea was starting to feel guilty for teasing him. After all, he had stopped when she'd asked him on the morning she'd fallen. So he was inhibited. We all had our little foibles, didn't we? She set the snifter on the floor outside the door and pulled it tightly shut again. "I'll leave the brandy out here for you. I'm afraid it took you too long to make up your mind about the massage," she bluffed. "I have to go now and check if the spaghetti water is boiling yet. But you just relax. I'll call you when dinner is ready."

Andrea's teasing hadn't worked out exactly to plan. She ended up back in the kitchen feeling rather small. She had made a guest in her home uncomfortable. She was shy, too, and could have been more understanding of Greg's conservatism. Maybe if she dressed up dinner a bit it would ease her conscience and take his mind off any immediate plans for retribution. Leaving her not-quite-boiling pot, she went into the living room. She put an extra log on the fire and flicked a hidden switch under the round coffee table, making the table magically rise to dining height. She found a pale blue linen cloth and went back to the kitchen to dig out her good china and crystal. Everyone needed a little spiritual uplift now and again, she rationalized. And this would be as good an occasion as any.

The heavy sterling silver her aunt had left her joined the table setting, and she stood back to admire the flash of fire reflected in her heavy cut-glass goblets. As she wandered back to begin the salad, she heard Tim whistling his way down the stairs. But as Andrea got out the lettuce, there was dead silence.

Suddenly Tim's resonant bass bellowed, "Karen! What have you done? Why am I being buttered up with a romantic dinner in the firelight? Did you put another dent in the car?"

Andrea tried hard to choke back her laughter while she stuffed lengths of stiff, straw-colored spaghetti into boiling water and went back to tearing lettuce. Tim had no idea how close to hitting the truth he was. But, he wasn't the one being buttered up. Karen's sounds of utter bewilderment as she came from their room to see what her spouse was yelling about were quickly followed by expressions of such indignation that Andrea had to stop and wipe tears of merriment from her eyes.

Tim and Karen converged on the kitchen together.

"What's going on?" they demanded in unison.

Andrea turned guileless eyes in their direction. "I merely thought the men deserved a little effort on our part in return for all their hard work. Do you realize, Karen, that between the two of them, they got the entire second story sealed? All it needs now is the final coat of paint. They deserve a little pampering, don't you agree?" And she reached to the radio and flicked on a classical station. A soothing violin concerto swirled through the first floor, adding, she hoped, to the general ambience she strove to create. Maybe she should dim the lights everywhere but the living room to disguise the remodeling mess. She could leave just enough light so that she wouldn't trip and land in the pot of spaghetti.

Karen eyed her lamblike expression suspiciously. Andrea knew she was doubting her own capability of pampering the male of the species. Coddling—at least the blatant type— wasn't her style. Tim reached to place the flat of his hand on Andrea's forehead and then his own, checking for fever. He shrugged his puzzlement. "Well, okay. If you're sure I'm not going to find a dent in the car or a new load of drywall that needs putting up, there's a bottle of wine I've been saving on the back porch. I'll get it."

"Andrea?" The single word was laden with inquisitive speculation.

"Hmm?"

"Is there anything I should know?"

"'Know'? Nothing that I can think of Karen. But if you're not too tired, you could slice the French bread and put the butter out to soften."

"There's more to this than meets the eye," Karen muttered, digging through a drawer to locate a bread knife. "I get the distinct impression I may be caught in a crossfire of some kind before the evening ends. Tim had better check that our life insurance is paid up."

"Coward," Andrea chided.

Twenty minutes later all was ready. Burgundy-hued wine had been poured into stemmed glasses. Pachelbel's Canon in D hung its moody presence over the room, and the fire cast a flickering light across the table, framing it and dropping the rest of the room into subdued shadow. Karen carried the food in while a cowardly Andrea sent Tim to roust Greg from the tub. Andrea, always going in two directions at once, decided to quarter some apples and sneak them on the burner to boil while they waited for Greg to make his appearance.

Chapter Three

"Sorry," Greg apologized as he emerged from the bathroom. "I actually fell asleep in the tub. I never realized how enervating a hot tub of water could be."

Andrea had never realized how enervating it could be to have a six-foot-two hunk of man come padding barefoot out of her bath in nothing but snugly fitting blue jeans. Wordlessly she measured the width of his strapping shoulders and analytically tried to gauge the amount of gently curling deep brown hair it took to cover the breadth of the chest in question with enough left over to taper down a flat stomach and disappear, still going strong, under the waistband of his faded jeans. Idly she wondered just exactly how far the band of hair went.

She turned red as the direction of her thoughts hit her conscious level. Turning back to her apples, she assured him, "It's all right, grab your shirt and come out to the living room. We're ready to eat."

He nodded his agreement and started to swing around to the bedroom when he noticed what she was doing. "Hey!

That's vinegar you're pouring into those apples. You must have picked up the wrong bottle."

Andrea snapped to. "What? Oh, no. It's all right. I've just developed a sudden craving for apple butter on toast for breakfast tomorrow. You need vinegar in apple butter."

"You make your own apple butter?" he questioned in astonishment.

"Yes."

He reiterated the facts, perhaps to make sure he had them right. "You bake Boston brown bread from scratch and make your own apple butter, but you can't add a little flour to meat drippings and come up with real gravy?" His whole body radiated disbelief.

How could one man be so hung up on her cooking methods? "Look, can you make a better gravy than what I turned out with that can of soup?"

"No," he admitted, then qualified, "But I've never really tried, either."

"Until you can, leave my culinary quirks out of any conversation we might have." Her lips clamped tightly on her pique. "If I ever find a good shortcut to apple butter or Boston brown bread, believe me, I'll use it." She turned back to stir the apples with more vigor than strictly necessary. Honestly, he might *look* good coming out of her bath, but educating this man back into the fun and joy of the real world would take someone with suicidal impulses.

He also seemed reluctant to fall under the spell she had so carefully staged. "My, my," he remarked on seeing the table. "From the ridiculous to the sublime. No one would ever guess from your taste in everyday crockery that you harbored a predilection toward Wedgwood and Waterford."

Karen and Tim eyed him warily as Tim held Karen's chair for her. Andrea was too resigned to hearing whatever came next to be surprised by a man's recognizing fine china and crystal on sight.

"How one person could embody so many diametrically opposed concepts is beyond me," Greg added.

Andrea dropped into her chair by herself before Tim could cover Greg's lack of social graces. She then explained rather shortly, "I used to work part-time at Marshall Field's. I collected one stem of Waterford per paycheck until I had service for eight. Then I started on china—piece by piece, month by month for three years before I had the whole set." She lovingly rubbed the rich cobalt-and-gold encrusted border on her plate. "I don't think I'll ever get tired of looking at it." The food was being ignored while Andrea warmed to one of her favorite topics. "Do you know what the difference is between fine and bone china?"

"She's going to get disgusting, and right before dinner, too," Greg warned.

Andrea ignored him and went blithely on. "The name does not refer simply to its color, but bone china has actual animal bone ground into its batter. When it's fired, it gets its characteristic white-white coloration. Fine china, on the other hand is a batter made with white clays. It has a higher concentration of feldspar. When it's fired, it takes on a creamy hue."

"What about porcelain?" Karen asked, interested.

"Now, porcelain is—"

"Uh, ladies? Could we possibly come back to this fascinating discussion at a later time? I'm starving. If you could, perchance, start the food around? It smells great," Tim said.

Andrea grimaced in apology. "Sorry, I tend to get carried away. I always found it fascinating to work in that section. I learned a lot, that's for sure." She helped herself to an abundant amount of pasta then passed the bowl to Greg.

Greg suspiciously eyed the spaghetti he had just spooned onto his plate and questioned, "Does this sauce have any mushrooms in it?"

"You have a mushroom fixation. What the hell is wrong with mushrooms that make you so totally irrational on the subject?"

"Mushrooms," he intoned darkly, "are a fungi."

"An *edible* fungi."

"A fungi, nonetheless."

"Oh, for heaven's sake. This is ridiculous. I don't know if there's mushrooms in there or not. If you can't live it up and take a chance, go out and read the label. The box is out in the garbage in the kitchen."

Greg's Italian heritage seemed to inspire an open rebellion. "The box? You mean you didn't make it? We're eating *store-bought* sauce? Candlelight can't camouflage taste, you know."

If the man didn't let up, he was going to be thrown out long before the week was out, sick or not. Sometime in the next ten minutes would be more like it, Andrea thought. He could just recover all by himself. "Spaghetti sauce takes hours of simmering to make properly," she informed him sweetly. "Did you happen to notice any simmering away while I was out looking for *your* apartment?"

Once again, his mind seemed to have stalled on what he saw as the only pertinent issue: "Store-bought sauce. That's revolting. Probably has mushrooms, too."

Andrea stared at him wide-eyed, her own food forgotten. How could anyone be so totally narrow-minded?

Karen, too, studied her uncle through slitted lids. From her expression it was clear she had never known her uncle to be so finicky before. It wasn't likely that medical school had changed him so radically, and years of cheap cafeteria eating were unlikely to develop such discerning taste buds. It was almost as though he were being difficult on purpose... trying to maintain an emotional distance.

"Try it, you may find you'll like it. This happens to be Fanny's Sauce, from an extremely popular Italian restaurant here in Evanston," Andrea explained as if to someone so dense that each word had to be spoken slowly and enunciated clearly. "They freeze it and sell it through the local groceries' freezer sections. I'm not sure if you can even get this anywhere else in the country. I bought it as a special treat. It's quite expensive."

Greg looked doubtful as he wound a single strand around the tines of his fork and chewed it dubiously. "It's okay," he allowed after swallowing and taking a sip of his wine.

Andrea leaned back in her chair and watched him pass the bowl on. "Well, hallelujah! He's going to condescend to eat our food."

Andrea noticed Karen looking at Tim in silent communication, as if pleading him to offer a new conversational topic.

As he doused his salad in the ranch-style dressing, Tim casually asked, "I noticed an envelope stuck in the door from the heating place. How much?"

Andrea wasn't too thrilled with this line of conversation either. "Too much," she sighed. "Fifteen hundred dollars."

Tim whistled. "Wow!"

"My reaction was a little more explicit."

"You weren't kidding that the kitchen would have to wait."

"What's really annoying," she grumbled, "is that the Kitchen Store is practically giving away one of their floor displays that was made to order for our kitchen. Solid oak, too. It even had a pantry cabinet with shelves on the doors, swing-out racks on piano hinges and more shelves behind those. They were holding it all for me until tomorrow night so that I could measure the kitchen and be sure." She sounded as if she were going deeper into mourning over her potential loss with each word. "I was really looking forward to a decent work area out there."

Greg had eaten half his pile of spaghetti with no further complaints. He slathered butter on a piece of bakery-fresh French bread as he spoke. "Couldn't you take out a home improvement loan or increase your mortgage? It seems a shame to miss out on such a good deal."

"I haven't got a mortgage to increase."

"Of course you do. Everybody gets a mortgage when they buy a house. It's those monthly payments you make."

"Not me. I don't believe in credit buying."

"How did you pay for the house then? Nobody pays cash for a house."

Andrea was aware of Tim holding his breath. He knew Andrea's background, having grown up next door to her; Greg did not. And Greg was trespassing on dangerous ground.

Instead of snapping off his head the way Tim was probably anticipating, Andrea responded with an only slightly strained smile. "My mother's sister, a charming lady, had no heirs. When she died a year ago, she left everything to me and my two sisters. We each chose some of her furniture to remember her by, and I used my share of the estate to buy this place. I've been slowly fixing it up ever since."

Greg looked around with new understanding. "The piano?"

"And this two-position coffee table we're eating at." She nodded. "Also some pieces I've got stored in the basement for the loft apartment."

"If you took out a home improvement loan or a small mortgage, the monthly payments wouldn't amount to much and you could have both the new kitchen and the boiler with enough left over to furnish the dining room," he pointed out reasonably.

Andrea's "No" came out with such vehemence that Greg was momentarily taken aback. He looked ready to pursue the argument when Andrea grabbed his dinner plate and piled it with the others.

"Hey! I wasn't finished yet."

"Yes, you were. You've had two helpings of store-bought sauce. I'm saving you from compromising your high standards and principles. Anyway, there's still dessert to come. You don't want to be too full, do you?"

"But there's still a little bit of spaghetti left in the bowl; it would be a shame to waste it."

"Have it for breakfast," Andrea advised as she whisked the bowl out of the line of fire.

Greg blanched at the thought. "Spaghetti for breakfast?"

"You didn't like what I made this morning," Andrea pointed out.

Greg called to her receding back as she carried the stack of dishes off, "What's wrong with eggs? What have you got against French toast or pancakes for breakfast? Something normal, for goodness' sake."

"Normality is a relative term," she called back. "If you'd break out of that rut you're in, widen your mental horizons, you could enjoy spaghetti for breakfast... or mushrooms at any time of day, for that matter." She was giving him a hard time for the heck of it. She wasn't all that sure she could face spaghetti at six o'clock in the morning, either. But it certainly was fun razzing him about it.

He was rising to follow her with another stack of dishes, but Tim detained him with a hand on his wrist while Karen took the dishes. "Don't pursue the loan bit, Greg. She's very sensitive about not buying on credit."

"A small loan would hardly be getting in over one's head," he argued equitably. "Especially if it's her only outstanding debt. Hell, I've got school loans up to my eyeballs, but I never could have been an M.D. without them."

"You know that and I know that. But her dad could probably fill out bankruptcy forms in his sleep. Her outlook has been colored by that for as long as I've known her, and we go back a way," he explained. "She's afraid it's like alcoholism or gambling—if she starts buying on credit, she won't be able to quit. Irrational, but there you are."

Greg felt compelled to argue further, "She's missing all kinds of tax advantages by allowing herself to overreact to her father like that." He sighed before capitulating. "Fine. I won't press it. It really isn't any of my business."

Tim's hand dropped away and Greg rose to follow Andrea out to the kitchen with the empty breadbasket in hand. "What's for dessert?" he called.

"Gâteau de Sara," came the unhesitating reply.

"What's a gattoe, and who's Sara? Some relative of Fanny's?"

"*Gâteau* is the French word for cake, and Sara may or may not be related to Fanny, I really don't know. She's the one nobody doesn't like. Sara Lee?"

"Out of a box from the freezer section," he grumbled on a low rumble.

"That's right," she trilled sweetly, flicking on the flame under the teakettle. "So cheer up. She makes a better Black Forest torte than I could even contemplate."

"I thought it was a *gâteau*."

"Same difference. It's still good, and I checked the label. No mushrooms, no soup."

"Thank heaven for small favors," he grumbled in mock relief. Grabbing the last slice of Boston brown bread, he trailed her back into the living room. At least with the bread he'd have *something* for dessert. He watched while she sliced the cake into even wedges. Cherries on chocolate cake. What mental midget had thought up that one? He viewed it from all angles while the other three participants made short work of theirs.

He tried a tentative forkful. It was a strange combination, but edible. And he wouldn't want to appear rude. He ate the whole thing before turning to his piece of Boston brown bread. It really was amazing, considering some of the strange concoctions that had been served since his arrival, how his appetite had gone from nonexistent to ravenous.

Karen looked stuffed. Greg knew the baby was big enough to crowd her stomach and not leave much room for a meal. He grinned as Karen leaned back in her chair and crossed her ankles instead of her knees to allow the baby as much room as possible. Karen looked from her uncle's empty plate to his eyes. He didn't have to be psychic to read the ironic expression. Greg flushed when he thought of the production his mother used to make of counting the silverware after a family meal just to be sure he hadn't inhaled any.

He winced as Karen attacked. "I can remember when you used to eat like that all the time. Years of bland cafeteria grilled cheeses and instant vanilla pudding have warped your taste buds. It's no wonder you've gotten so thin. Who could thrive on that junk? With a frame as large as yours, you should put on at least ten to fifteen pounds, maybe more. What you need—" Karen paused to ensure his attention and to emphasize her next words "—is a wife to take you in hand. Yep." She nodded in agreement with her own analysis while Tim looked nervous and took a hurried sip of water. Greg eyed her skeptically.

"A good woman," she continued, "would broaden your horizons in more ways than just food. You've had a very narrowly focused life out of necessity for so long, you're going to need help breaking loose and branching out. You know what's wrong with you?"

Her uncle shook his head, taking a hearty bite out of his brown bread.

"Being an M.D., I'm sure you've heard of babies who literally die for lack of love and touching."

Greg shook his head, positively this time.

Karen leaned forward to point at him in emphasis. "You're in danger of that as an adult. That's why it's taking you so long to recover from this bout of hepatitis. You need someone to bond with before you waste away." And she leaned back in the chair again, very pleased with her analysis of the situation.

Before Greg could swallow the lump of bread now uncomfortably lodged in his throat and begin to refute her claim, Tim decided to join the cause. "I know a likely candidate who could volunteer for the position. She suffers from the same problem, only she doesn't know it yet."

Andrea stared at him wide-eyed. "How can you talk about your own sister that way? Lisa would murder you in cold blood if she knew you were putting her on the auction block that way."

"I wasn't referring to Lisa." Tim looked at Andrea pointedly.

"Oh, no. Ooh, no." She reached forward to clatter her cup down in its saucer before pounding a choking Greg on the back. "Look what you've done! You're supposed to be helping him recover and now you're going to have to save him from choking instead. Someone to bond with. How ridiculous! It will be on your conscience if he dies," she said with a steely-eyed glare at Tim, her displeasure with him evident.

Greg was still sputtering but managed to draw in a struggling breath and wheeze, "Stop hitting me. You've managed to dislodge the bread, there's no need to shake loose every organ in my body."

"Rotten ingrate." She gave him one final healthy whack before crossing her arms indignantly and sitting back in her chair.

Between little residual coughs, Greg spoke. "I admit it's probably time I found someone to carry on the family name. I'm aware that I'm the last male in a long succession of Rennolds."

Andrea's glare let him know her opinion of his callous approach to love and marriage. All to be done in the line of familial genetic duty, she supposed. Pity the poor girl stuck with this clod. She hoped he and his little paragon of a wife produced nothing but girls. Then she determinedly stifled the warm chill that came over her at the thought of carrying Greg's babies.

"However, when I take a wife, it's not going to be some pseudoliberated woman who couldn't cook if soup manufacturers went out of business and who'd burned all her bras—"

"I've never burned a bra in my life," Andrea gasped in outrage, not even noticing how Tim and Karen perked up at the reference to her underwear. "I just didn't choose to wear one this morning. There are at least three in my drawer. You were in my room when I got dressed and I couldn't—"

"Are you implying you would like to audition for the job?"

"Absolutely not. There isn't enough gold in Fort Knox to..."

Greg waved away her rantings with a negligent hand. "The woman I marry, as I was saying, will be gentle and petite. Into baking bread." His gaze was caught by the slice of homemade Boston brown bread he was waving in the air to underline his words. Carefully, he placed it down on the edge of his saucer before continuing. "The kids will be scrubbed and shiny, ready to be tucked in when I arrive home, and then I'll share a romantic candlelit dinner for two with my wife before we go to bed ourselves."

"Brother, talk about fantasy. That kind of 1950 paragon is hard to find nowadays. A lot of women either want to or have to work to help supplement their husband's income and are too tired to wait on anybody like that. Besides," Andrea concluded dismissingly, "you haven't got the personality to draw that side of a woman out. She'd hit you with her empty soup cans before putting dinner on the table."

"There won't *be* any empty soup cans in *my* wife's kitchen." Greg glared at Andrea, but further remarks were forestalled by the chiming doorbell.

Andrea declared the evening's attempt at creating a mellow atmosphere a failure by flicking a switch on her way to answer the door. The room was suddenly bathed in stark light and its occupants blinked in an effort to adjust to the glare.

Shivering on her doorstep, she discovered her next-door neighbor's son, eight-year-old Jimmy McKnight, who looked up soulfully, an entreating expression on his freckled countenance.

"Jimmy! You're not allowed out after supper. Is anything wrong?" She ushered him quickly into the warm living room, and in her momentary concern, did not notice the small yellow and blue rectangular box clutched to his chest.

The child shook his head mutely in response to her question. No, nothing was wrong. Andrea eyed him speculatively. He had only recently begun opening up to her when they were alone. Now, with so many people in the room, Jimmy's tongue was not about to loosen its grip from the roof of his mouth. He studied the polished golden oak planking beneath his feet for a full sixty seconds before silently proffering the small cardboard box.

"What have to got there, Jimbo?" Andrea inquired more softly as she read the label. "Official Cub Scout Pinewood Derby Kit. And your name on it, hmm? I didn't know you were a Cub Scout."

He nodded vigorously. "Just this year," he whispered in barely audible tones.

Andrea read further. "It says here this is supposed to be a father-son project. Can't your dad do this with you?" Warning bells were beginning to clang in her head. She didn't know anything about building cars, for heaven's sake, and once again, she knew what was coming.

She had to lean closer to hear the barely audible explanation. "He has to work the night shift all this month, so we're never home at the same time. Mom said she'd do it with me, but she's never sawed or hammered anything before," he confessed in a rush. "I've seen you hammerin', though." He looked up from his intent study of his scuffed and stained sneaker tips, glanced shyly at her and quickly reverted his gaze back to the red and blue striped canvas shoe. "I was hopin'... Mom said I could ask... Maybe you would, you know..."

Andrea's heart sank to her toes. Yeah, she knew all right. She knew she was trapped again, for one thing. She'd kill Maureen when she saw her in the morning. Any car she might make would be an unmitigated disaster. She knew that with a deadly certainty. She turned the box in her hands, pretending to study the label again and glanced surreptitiously at the anxious visage before her. Why did he have to have so many little freckles sprinkled across his nose? And how had he gotten so pale and orphanish looking already? Damn, it was happening again. She wouldn't be able to turn him down.

Karen had been clearing the table and Andrea now headed for the vacated area. "Let's dump the contents of the box out on the table and see what's here, okay?" Maybe it wouldn't be so bad and she could talk Tim into—

Her hopes were summarily dashed as Tim rose and stretched languidly. "I'll get the dishes and then I absolutely have to get some studying done. It won't have done you any good to have taken us in if I flunk the tortes exam." He was letting her know he didn't have time to help her out of this one. Her spirits sank further. Flipping open the top of the box, she tilted it down to the table and gave a gentle shake. Out came a block of pine, four nails, and four wheels—also a set of directions, which she gingerly unfolded, fingering it with all the distaste of a registered letter from the Internal Revenue Service.

"I'll help you," Jimmy was saying eagerly. "All you hafta do is tell me what to do. Dad says I'm a big help to him, handin' him nails and stuff. Oh, and Mom says she has some drapery weights we can use."

Andrea had been looking morosely back and forth from the directions to the chunk of unfinished wood, but his last words broke through her shell-shocked state. Drapery weights? What the heck was she supposed to do with those? Frantically, she went back to the directions. She had to cut the wood twice, and on an angle, no less. Weights... weights... There it was. The finished car was to weigh no more than four ounces, but should be weighted to come as close to the allowed weight as possible without exceeding it. The heavier the car, the faster it would travel down the track. Wonderful. Nowhere did it say how one was to attach these indispensable weights.

Closing her eyes, the backs of her lids provided the screen for a Technicolor nightmare. Jimmy's car was rolling in slow motion down the track, spitefully shucking off one wheel at a time in a disorderly progression, each one bouncing off with a defiant *ping* until all four had been heartlessly cast off. Now it came to a grinding halt halfway down the speedway while the other Cubs' cars flashed by, streaking onto the finish line in a blaze of sawdust.

The vision cleared, and Andrea gave her head an impatient shake to clear away the fading image. Painfully she turned to Jimmy. "Uh, let's go on down to the basement, okay? We can go through the toolbox and see what we'll need."

She turned to Karen and instructed in an aside, "If you still have any energy whatsoever, I think there's some of that cookie dough left from the other day in the back of the refrigerator. Don't let Tim see what you're doing until it's too late. He'll have a fit if he sees you greasing the cookie sheet before he's even finished cleaning the last batch of pans. Don't bother with the food coloring. A little sugar sprinkled on top will be fine."

Karen nodded sympathetically while Andrea bent to gather the various nails and wheels, directions and wood. She squared her shoulders and motioned to the small boy in the patched jeans and cotton T-shirt emblazoned with a cartooned elf and the logo Cookie Elves Believe in the Cubs, to precede her.

Leaning over to whisper in Karen's ear, she curtly directed, "I don't really care what that unfeeling hulk in the kitchen says, get me those cookies. I'm going to need them to raise my stock with Jimmy after he sees what kind of incompetent clod he's aligned himself with." She straightened up and fatalistically saluted Karen while rolling her eyes. "We who are about to die... and all of that."

Karen laughed. "Never mind any last words. Go down and face the firing squad like the big brave girl we know you are. You'll do fine."

"That only shows how little you really know me, even after living in the same house all this time," Andrea muttered in resignation.

Greg watched the delicate sway of Andrea's gray velour-clad hips as they receded into the rear of the house. He spoke contemplatively, almost as if he had forgotten Karen's presence. "Interesting. The longer I'm here, the more of an enigma she becomes. I'm beginning to suspect that under that gruff exterior a heart beats after all. Maybe not twenty-four karat, but eighteen at any rate. She has no child, yet runs a Brownie troop. You and Tim pay no rent. She's said nothing to me about money, either. A blind man could see she's worried over disappointing that little kid. Interesting."

Karen leaned forward to place her neatly tapered fingers flat against the blue linen cloth. Her own brown eyes met her uncle's in a direct, no-nonsense fashion. "Don't make the mistake of letting Andrea's bark turn you off to the inner beauty of the person. She's sandpapery, but only on the outside. She didn't have to let Tim and me stay here. Plenty of other people commiserated with us on our bad luck, then figured their duty had been done with lip service. Not Andrea. She's given us a way to keep our pride. Tim is well aware that Mom didn't really approve of him, and we both hated to give her the chance to say 'I told you so.' Sure, Tim works around here when he can, but we don't begin to put in what we get out. And Andrea honestly doesn't care. Tim's been like a brother to her. They've been close since they were five years old. The moment she met me, she made it clear I could place any demands on her that a member of her family might."

Much to her uncle's surprise, Karen's eyes glistened damply as she continued, although her gaze never wavered. "I can't tell you what that meant to me, having lived most of my life as an overprotected only child. And as for kids, she loves them. She wasn't kidding when she said she had demanded our child in return for room and board. One of the only stipulations she made when we came here to live was that anytime we went out after the baby came, she would get to baby-sit. She is truly a caring, loving person."

Greg was surprised by Karen's outburst—not only by the depth of emotion Andrea seemed to evoke in her friends, but also by the feeling of hurt he felt at the transfer of an allegiance that had always been his. Suddenly he was the outsider in Karen's life. It was food for thought.

"It was nice of you all to host me for the weekend," he attempted. "But tomorrow I plan to get a room at the Orrington until I can find an apartment. I don't want to take advantage."

Karen flicked her hand to show what she thought of that. "You have to admit, three decent meals a day for the past two days haven't done you any harm. You're already looking better, although I like to think that's from being around your scintillating niece rather than Andrea's cooking." She dimpled easily at him, her former earnestness submerged. "Tim and I will make it up to Andrea eventually, don't worry. Just be nice to her."

Greg gave her a disparaging glance, letting her know that not only did he believe her to be a lost cause, but also that he could see right through her. "For your information, I am not quite the dirty so-and-so you seem to believe. I have been too busy studying to leave much of a trail of broken hearts behind me."

"With your looks?" Karen asked in a disbelieving tone.

"Looks don't get you grades, unfortunately." He rose majestically from the table, towering over Karen. "Be that as it may, *I* was a Cub Scout, and *my* cars always placed high in the Pinewood Derbies. If you will excuse me, I will go rescue Jimmy from the clutches of that *Brownie* leader before his car is irreparably damaged." "Brownie" came out as a dirty word, beneath the dignity of a Cub Scout's association.

Karen hummed a little tune as she followed Greg through to the kitchen. Greg was too preoccupied to remember that Karen had always hummed when scheming.

Chapter Four

By eight o'clock that evening, the block of natural pine had made remarkable progress. It had been carefully molded into its proper shape and then sanded with not one or two, but three progressively finer grades of sandpaper. Now it was clamped in a vise like a turtle sprawled on its back. Andrea watched Greg's large, blunt fingers make a delicate adjustment to the wide-bladed bit he had inserted into the drill. Then he began to exactly drill out the precise area he required on the car's understructure. Greg explained to Jimmy as he worked that this way, the weights could be hidden up in the underside, and not mar the lines of the finished racer.

Andrea had concluded that Greg had missed his calling, that his agile fingers might have been put to better use as a carpenter or sculptor, when Karen called down the stairs, "I'm bringing milk and cookies. You'll have to eat them fast, though. Jimmy's mother called, and she wants him home. It's a school night, she says."

"Don't do the stairs, Karen," Andrea called back. "We'll be right up."

"Not to worry. I have to give my seal of approval to the product of the last few hours' labors anyway." With that, she started down the steep steps. It was an interesting challenge, as the stairs were narrow and her stomach large. Her oversize tummy kept her from holding the plastic tray with its plate of sugar-dusted cookies and half-filled Dixie cups of milk anywhere near her body. Instead, she had to hold it out where it interfered with her already diminished sense of balance.

Andrea was too busy admiring the ease with which Greg handled himself around the tool bench to notice Karen's struggling descent. Her first inkling of a problem came with Karen's smothered shriek as, right at the bottom, victory almost hers, she lost her balance and sat down hard on the second step. The cacophony of the clattering tray on the cement floor, the spreading puddle of milk, and the flying cookie chunks made it seem far worse a catastrophe than it really was.

Andrea turned, frozen in horror as she took in Karen's shocked expression. She heard herself calling as if from a distance, "Oh, my God! Peggy! You'll lose the baby. Oh, my God!"

Greg, on his way to help Karen up, looked at Andrea strangely: but more concerned with getting Karen out of the spilled milk, he let his curiosity over Andrea's scream of "Peggy" wait.

"Oh, my God! We'll have to call the doctor right away. The emergency room... No, she probably shouldn't be moved. An ambulance, that's it. They have radio connections now that go right to the hospital in them."

From his crouched position, Greg urged, "Relax, Andrea. All she did was sit down. I'm a doctor, remember? She's going to be fine."

"But the baby..."

"Pregnant women do stuff like this all the time," he assured her. "Their sense of gravity changes and babies sometimes put pressure on the nerve at the top of the leg, causing the leg to go out from under them. It's not a big deal. Those babies are so well cushioned, it would take a whole lot more than just sitting down hard to shake them loose. Really, she's okay."

Just to be sure, he checked Karen's legs and arms before helping her up. "Let's go on up now. I've got my stethoscope upstairs. We'll listen to the fetal heart tones and put Miss Worrywart's mind to rest."

Andrea escorted a tongue-tied Jimmy up the stairs where she found a small cache of unbroken cookies. Trying not to be too obvious, she breathed a sigh of relief as she pressed a handful on him and hustled the eight-year-old out the door, waving goodbye before hurrying to Karen's bedroom.

Breathlessly she took in the scene. Karen lay ensconced on her bed decked in a frilly white nightgown with lace up to her chin, a solicitous Tim paying court on one side while Greg tucked his blood-pressure cuff and stethoscope back into his traditional black doctor's bag on the other. The martyred expression on Karen's face would have done credit to a queen in a Victorian melodrama, and Andrea was immediately on her guard.

"The baby's okay?" she warily questioned.

Greg nodded. "Yep. Judging by the amount of activity going on down there right now, Karen had better put in a supply of track shoes just to keep up with this kid after he's born. She thinks she might have pulled a muscle, though."

"Oh? Where?" Andrea's gut-wrenching fears were rapidly dissolving into frissons of suspicion. There was something peculiar about the current arrangement of Karen's facial features that might lead a less trusting sort to doubt the reality of the damage in question.

"Ooh, my wrist," Karen moaned piteously, hanging the offended limb out for inspection. "I think it's sprained."

"Perhaps we ought to get it checked at the hospital," Tim said worriedly.

"Oh, I'm sure it'll be all right if I just don't use it for a few days. They can't X-ray it anyway. I'm pregnant, remember?" Karen quickly broke in before turning oddly complacent eyes on her uncle. "But you know how hard it is to do things one-handed, and I do have a lot to do this week."

She pretended not to hear Andrea's strangled "Like what?"

"I don't suppose, since you're free this week anyway, that you'd consider sticking around a few more days? Just to kind of be here, if you know what I mean. That fall has made me quite wary of being by myself. What if it happens while I'm alone?" she questioned in what sounded like smug satisfaction rather than real worry.

"Ah, Karen, my love. You forget I've known you for a long, long time. Sorry, but tomorrow I go to a hotel." He snapped his black bag shut, but was prevented from leaving.

Tim broke in sheepishly, "Actually, I'm a little shook-up by all this myself. If you're going to the hotel because you're worried about outstaying your welcome, I'd really appreciate it if you'd reconsider. This has got to be nicer than any cramped hotel room until you find an apartment. And Andrea doesn't mind, do you, Andrea?"

Andrea's arms were crossed in front of her body, and she rocked from heel to toe and back again as she eyed Karen speculatively. "Why do I get the distinct impression that I'm being had?"

"I'm sure I wouldn't know." Karen sniffed. "I would never sink to manipulation, even if it would be in the best interests of some other party."

"Hah. I'm only agreeing to this for Tim's peace of mind and because my own Red Cross certificate expired two months ago—although considering the shape the doctor in question is in, I ought to get it renewed. Who's going to doctor the doctor?"

"The doctor doesn't need doctoring," Greg retorted, "only rest, which would be a more likely possibility elsewhere. However, since my presence has been so graciously requested, how can I say no?" He turned to Andrea. "When you're done coddling the noninvalid here, come into the living room and we'll discuss the price of room and board."

Andrea waited until Greg had firmly closed the door behind his departing back before threatening her friend on the bed. "If you've conjured up some crazy idea of propinquity and wedding bells, you can just forget it. He's not my type."

"He's awfully good-looking..." Karen tempted.

"Now you listen to me. I will dump you out the front door right on your sprained wrist if you start throwing him at me, or me at him, for that matter."

"I won't have to," Karen said in satisfied tones. "Things will happen all by themselves if I can just manage to keep you around each other long enough to give it time. I can feel it in my bones."

"That, no doubt, is the onset of rheumatism, and this is not going to work. We'll be at each other's throats again in no time."

Karen lay back against the pillow, placing the back of a languid wrist over her closed eyes. "Tim," she complained, "I'm getting a headache. Make her go into the living room and discuss rent with Greg, will you? But you stay here with me, in case I black out."

"Oh, for heaven's sake. I'm going. Just don't say I didn't warn you it wouldn't work. You'll really have a migraine with all of us living on top of each other the next week or two."

"Oh, it could be months before an apartment becomes available, you know. A really nice one in the proper area, that is," Karen advised.

Andrea could hear Tim's amused voice as she went down the small hallway. "I hope you know what you're doing. She looks ready to chew nails."

Darn right, Andrea thought, fuming. *I'm not so totally without saving graces that I have to resort to prospective husbands being hog-tied and held so I can grow on them like some darn piece of lichen on the side of a darn tree. Those two will soon realize they're beating a dead horse on this issue,* she decided. *I don't need a man, I don't want a man, and I'm certainly not going to allow them to force-feed me that... that emotionally backward... jerk!* The realization that she could quite easily come to love that particular jerk galled her, feeding her righteous indignation with each step until by the time she reached the living room, she was virtually stomping and the look on her face would have quelled a lesser man.

"Women who smoke are terribly unattractive, you know."

"I don't smoke."

"You must. Furthermore, it looks as if you exhale through your ears. There are big gray plumes of noxious smoke billowing out of them right now. Calm down and let's talk. We need to get to know each other a little bit."

"Why?" Andrea demanded, viciously poking at the flagging fire only to jump back from the maelstrom of bursting sparks she had set loose.

Greg pulled her back from the spitting blaze and quickly set the mesh curtain over the opening. He pushed her down on the sofa, directing, "Sit down and listen to me."

Andrea struck out against that indefinable chemistry that attracted her to him. "You don't have to stay here, you know. There's no reason we have to coddle that crazy woman's whims just because she's pregnant. Ice cream and pickles at two in the morning, fine. But no way is she going to saddle me with her idea of the perfect mate. The vagaries of expectant motherhood will only take her so far. We don't even like each other." She crossed her arms obstinately and glared at him.

She panicked at Greg's endearing grin, feeling the noose tighten yet another notch. "I don't know," he said. "This place and all you loonies that populate it are starting to grow on me. It's what I feared, you know."

"*Us* loonies!" Andrea sniffed.

"Yeah, you loonies," Greg agreed. "And before you go getting all indignant again, let's talk about this rationally."

Andrea's face was set in stubborn mutiny although she remained silent. Greg settled his tall frame next to hers on the plumply pillowed sofa and threw a companionable arm along the rise of the back, behind but not quite touching Andrea's shoulders. She could feel the heat of his body jump the short distance to her own and, oddly, it produced a shivery chill that feathered its cold fingers down the length of her spine and back up again.

"Look at it this way," Greg urged. "This could work to both our advantages. I could use some decent meals, and I can't cook. Going out for every meal would be a pain while I'm still feeling so tired. You, on the other hand," Greg continued in his calming deep bass, "why, you get a bit of extra income at a time when you could use it, without that much extra effort. You cook anyway, and you could throw my laundry in with yours without a big deal. Karen and Tim will be moving upstairs by the end of the week, so I can just take their room. And while I'm well aware that Karen thinks she is being terribly cunning, I also think Tim might feel a little better if there was a doctor in the house, so to speak."

"You'd have to take your turns at the jobs around here; I don't feel like playing glorified maid," Andrea stipulated crossly.

Greg cajoled her teasingly. "It won't be so bad, and we might even have a little fun at Karen's expense," he whispered.

"How?"

"Watch this," he instructed before he gently pulled her into his arms and began lowering his mouth to hers.

"What do you think you're doing?" Andrea squeaked and then winced. Had that high-pitched squeal actually been her voice?

"Shh, relax." His mouth made firm contact with hers. She lay rigidly in his arms, too stunned by the suddenness of the maneuver to struggle. He lightly nibbled her generous lower lip while his arm adjusted her position in his lap to maximum advantage. Then his capable doctor's hands began drawing teasing, light circles along her upper arms and across her collarbone. The sensuous feel as he moved against her velvety velour jogging top added to the power and effect of his touch, making her shudder and relax.

"What are you doing?" she moaned in much different, lower tones.

"Just enjoy," he muttered against her lips as he continued marauding the treasures of her mouth. "I certainly am." His tongue questingly probed the tight line of her clenched lips, and she parted them, allowing him free access to the damply dark plunder beyond, and she was shocked by her own actions. Never in her twenty-four years had she ever experienced anything with the rampaging power of this kiss. She felt hot and then shivery cold in rapid succession and her arms, with a will all their own, moved to a spot low on his back.

Not that she was much of a judge, but it seemed that Greg was not exempt from the powerful current she felt flowing through their bodies. His breath had noticeably quickened. One hand had roamed to a position just under her breast, allowing its weight to rest against him. And Andrea, who had never before been interested enough in any man to allow intimacies past the mandatory good-night kiss, found her whole body tingling in anticipation of some unknown end. For the first time, she was fighting her bodily instincts. It was all she could do to prevent her own hand from moving his up the last few inches to its throbbing goal.

There was the oddest, almost *compulsive* type of budding feeling building down deep in her very being. She could feel her pulse racing, her blood rushing to bring its flush to her normally delicate pearl skin tones and act as witness to the kiss's potent effect.

She leaned back in his arms to search his face in wonderment. It was a humbling experience to realize that she, who had always sworn never to be used to satisfy a man's baser instincts, had a few base instincts of her own. Much more of this, and *she'd* be pleading with *him* to finish what he'd started.

"My!" Andrea muttered in amazement. "I'd ask where you learned to do that, but my tender sensibilities would probably be shocked, so don't tell me. I'm sure I don't want to know."

"It was rather good, wasn't it?"

A door clicked shut in the background. Greg grinned roguishly and tipped his head to the side. "Hear that? That was Karen going back to report to Tim on our progress as a loving duo."

Andrea looked shocked. "She was listening?"

"Mmm."

"You devastated me like that because she was listening and you wanted to shock her?" Greg's expression grew warily rueful as he nodded again. "I hope she turns into a pillar of salt, just like the biblical people who turned back for a final look at Sodom and Gomorrah."

"It was pretty good as far as kisses go, but I'm not sure it would be in quite the same category as the fall of Sodom and Gomorrah."

A dazed Andrea was having a little trouble taking it all in. "I'm sitting here shattered, and it was all some kind of game. You did this to me to teach your niece some kind of lesson. I hope you both rot in—"

"Now hold on a minute. That was how it *started*. I admit I thought it would be fun to take her for a ride and let her think there was something between us for a while, but now I'm not so sure it would work. You're not the only one feeling a little shattered right now. I initiated that kiss to make Karen realize her error, but it seems to have backfired. I may have to credit her with more insight than I thought possible."

He sank back into the sofa's cushions and pulled Andrea down beside him, tucking her head onto his shoulder, his left arm comfortably resting along the wary, slightly trembling breadth of her shoulders while his free hand played with a tendril of lustrous ebony hair that curled across the swell of her firm breast.

Andrea was appalled to discover her own delicately-boned hand testing the texture of the silky brown hair protruding from the top of his hunter-plaid flannel shirt. As she watched in a detached manner, she spoke almost reverently. "It boggles the mind to think what might have happened here. I almost threw myself at you. I have never thrown myself at a man. Never." She took in a long breath before slowly expelling it. "I've just had a rather startling revelation into my character, and I'm not sure I ought to be alone in the same room with you for a while."

Her voice was so incredulous, as though she couldn't quite believe what had just happened, that Greg laughed and hugged her to him. "It was rather dynamic, wasn't it? We'll try to exercise more discretion in the future." It seemed to her that he did the exact opposite as he instituted a series of butterfly-light kisses along her hairline and down the slender length of her neck. Finally he snuggled closer to her body and lay his head next to hers on the sofa back. Brushing her hair away to expose the tender nape of her neck, he kissed her there, too. "I knew it would be fun teasing Karen, I just didn't realize how much fun. You all were right earlier; I do need to loosen up."

"I'm not sure jumping feetfirst into an inferno is exactly what we had in mind, especially since you seem intent on taking me with you. Couldn't you start off by learning to like mushrooms?"

"Uh-uh," Greg returned languidly, nibbling on her earlobe. "This particular portion of your anatomy is infinitely superior to any mushroom." His warm breath gusting down her neck made her shudder. Not realizing the cause of her chills, he pulled her closer to share his body heat. "Besides, any good Scout knows how to tend a flame without anyone getting burned."

"Yeah? Well I've got news for you. If you don't quit fanning the flames, the entire sofa is going to go up in smoke."

There was no response, but his tongue had stopped inflicting its slow torture on her suddenly erotic earlobe. She pulled her head back to bring him into focus. His eyes were closed, his generous lips slightly parted. His steady breathing gave it away. This was not a man trying to control his flaming passion, but rather a man who had fallen sound asleep, dousing the flames by rolling on them with his body, like a good Scout.

So much for her uncontrollably passionate appeal. Andrea grimaced as she pushed against his body, now heavily slumped upon her in its relaxed slumber. She would have been insulted by the turn of events had she not also been relieved. His body shifted enough to take off the heavy pressure, but not enough to gain her release. Even if she called to Karen and Tim, they probably wouldn't hear her through their closed door, and she rather thought the enjoyment they would display at her predicament would not be counterbalanced by the benefits of release. It would be better to suffer in silence than suffer under their knowing looks for the next few days. At least now she could honestly say she'd slept with a man.

Chuckling at her wayward thoughts, she leaned as far as she could, just managing to hook a finger into the gay profusion of multicolored woven yarns making up a grannypatch afghan that hung barely within reach across the back of the sofa. Awkwardly, she managed to spread it over them with her one free hand, hoping that, combined with his body warmth next to her, it would be enough to see them through the night.

She needn't have worried. Waking once during the night, she knew the house was cool but was amazed at how warm she was. She, who normally bundled for bed during the colder months with layers of wool socks and quilted robes, actually had to stick an arm and a foot out from under the crocheted blanket in an effort to lower her body temperature. At that moment, a large plus in marriage's favor made its way into her consciousness. Warmth in winter, what heaven! Greg's male heat in such close proximity was infinitely superior to any brand of electric blanket she'd tried—the problem being, of course, what did one do with a spouse during the summer months? You couldn't fold up a man and put him on the closet shelf with a mothball or two until fall. After giving the problem her due consideration, she decided thoughtfully that if things got too bad, one could try ceiling fans or twin beds. She wondered if many married couples traded beds with the seasons. She'd have to think about that some other time. There were more pressing problems at the moment—such as what to do about the top that had ridden up her back and the strange hand that had burrowed and trespassed onto forbidden territory.

It would have to be done without waking him up. She didn't want him to be aware of what had been allowed during her sleep. It was bad enough to live with his knowledge of her earlier wanton response. There was no point adding fuel to the fire. Gently, gently, she tried to ease his hand out so she could pull her top back down. But it was not to be. Annoyed in his sleep at losing his warm sanctuary, he grumbled, twisted and turned, then grabbed her with two hands before shaping her like a pillow underneath his head, cradling his tousled hair on her trembling breasts and jamming one hand back up her shirt, higher than before.

And she thought she was warm before. Darn! She was so hot now she felt his head as an almost suffocating weight clamping down on her lungs as they labored to bring in some air. Her breathing took the form of short gasps, and she watched as his head rose and fell against her.

Her imagination began to take flight, pulling her right along in its wake. She could see him slowly wakening, his inhibitions still suppressed in his half-slumberous state. She could literally *feel* the swelling in her breasts begin and grow at the thought of his hand, which now rested casually at the base of her breast, moving to take up a gentle, rhythmic cadence against the tender pink tip eagerly waiting for his warm, slightly roughened palm. She could see his languorous dark eyes studying her face before centering on her slightly parted lips. She imagined delicately licking her expectant, pouting lips with the tip of her tongue, inviting him to follow as it disappeared again from sight. His own mouth would slowly lower to claim hers, their heated breaths mixing and fusing into one. The feelings shooting through her were so intense, they could only be described, however incongruously, as *excruciatingly* pleasurable.

By now Andrea's entire leg was out from under the blanket in a fruitless attempt to control a bodily thermostat gone thoroughly haywire. This was awful. One kiss and she had turned shamelessly wanton. What was she to do? This was not the type of man she had foreseen for herself. Not at all. What woman could boast of falling for the original stick-in-the-mud? He viewed life with such narrow vision. How could she be happy with someone who had lost his joy of living and sense of humor while picking up his medical degree? The M.D. had cost him, but was she willing to pick up the tab? Heavens, she wanted to. She could possibly view it as a great work of mercy. Saving the world from another humorless doctor.

A sudden slight snore from the head resting on her chest brought Andrea back from her prurient flights of fancy. She listened to the dull sound of his slight grunt and watched his two fingers deal with the end of his twitching nose before he buried his face once more into her chest. Sometimes works of mercy had their own rewards.

Andrea pushed her other foot out from under the afghan, and giving in to a little whim, threaded slender fingers through the thick tangle of his cropped curls. In his sleep he would never notice the hand cradling him to her bosom.

She gave conscious attention to slowing her breathing rate, and it was a credit to her persevering willpower that she gradually drifted back into a deep slumber, not awakening again until her ever-faithful internal alarm went off at precisely five forty-five.

As she contemplated how to squirm her way out of the intimately enmeshed tangle of arms and legs, Greg's long lashes began to flicker. Andrea, who had never had the opportunity to watch a man awaken before, observed, fascinated as the lean body next to her gradually took on the more hardened muscle tones of alert awareness. "Hi." He grinned sleepily. "You make a great pillow. Soft and comfortable," he complimented. He was lying on his side next to her, having lifted his head from her breasts to watch her while he spoke.

"Thank you. The pleasure was all yours." She rubbed the sleep from her eyes and stretched, her arms high over her head. "You weigh—" She stopped in midsentence as Greg, who had successfully maintained his perch on the narrow couch all night, was knocked from its safe confines by her hyperextended elbows and fell with a yelp and accompanying dull thud to the floor below.

"Hey! If you wanted me to move, all you had to do was ask. I'm going to have to warn any boyfriends you bring around that you have all the earmarks of a potential husband-beater."

Andrea was too happy to point out the flaws in his reasoning. "First of all, I tried for a good twenty minutes last night to get you to move so that I could go to bed. You, sir, are dead to the world when you sleep and are an equally deadweight to try to budge. Furthermore, if you think I'm stupid enough to bring any prospective mates home while

I've got my own private loony tunes going on here, you have more than one screw loose up there." She tapped the top of his head to lend significance to her words. "What man would understand not only the general chaos around here, but a platonic rooming arrangement with a doctor type who my mother would refer to as having prospects?"

Greg thought about that while Andrea sat up, combing her tapered fingers through her hair. Somehow the thought of his being the cause of other prospective suitors' taking a hike for a while didn't seem to upset him terribly.

"Yes," he said, "I can see that it might be hard to explain." He was speaking a little too brightly to convey any truly remorseful feelings on the matter, but he did make a generous offer. "However, I'd be more than willing to try to clarify it for you. Is there anyone special in your life to whom I should worry about defending your honor?" The question was put casually, but there was a certain underlying tension.

Andrea studied him disgustedly. Men could be so obvious at times. "No, there is no one special I would care to have you explain yourself to. But don't get your hopes up; this relationship stays platonic. Yesterday evening meant nothing. A pleasant little interlude." With all the lies she was spewing out this morning, it was fortunate there was no Uncle Geppetto in her life. She rose and turned toward the door. "Now, if you'll excuse me, I have to get ready for work."

Greg watched from his seat on the floor as she flounced from the room. He murmured into the slightly perfumed vacuum left behind, "'Pleasant interlude,' my foot. There is one hell of a responsive woman hiding behind that brave rhetoric, and I fully intend to uncover and claim her." Then he rose and absently brushed the lint from the back of his pants before heading for the kitchen with vague thoughts of preventing a repeat of yesterday morning's breakfast.

A dab of margarine was heating in the bottom of the skillet while Greg whipped several eggs with a fork. Andrea stepped from the bathroom, dressed for work. His eyes flared with a deeper, more brilliant mahogany, and his mouth dropped open in his surprise. He mutely studied her. Her shining blue-black hair was clipped in a loose knot at the back of her head with an oversize tortoiseshell barrette and she wore a jazzily striped white, charcoal and black form-fitting leotard with leg-hugging black tights that showed every curve of her gently muscled thighs and calves.

"Wow!" he muttered, respect evident in his tone. "I wondered what was hiding under all those loose sweats you've favored since I've been here. I had no idea it would be so...so..." He stopped, momentarily at a loss for an adequate descriptive term.

She looked disparagingly at him. "Considering where you and your hand spent last night it's a little hard to believe you don't know exactly what was under the sweats." She sounded piqued. "And don't expect me to believe I'm suddenly irresistible. I don't buy it."

"Obviously I missed out on something pretty spectacular while I slept. Can I have an instant replay?"

"Oh, for crying out loud, what a—"

"Besides," he went on bluntly, "you yourself intimated that your breasts were not your best feature." He glanced meaningfully at the flare of her hips and the well-defined curve of her calf. He poured the bowl of scrambled eggs into the pan, his gaze still firmly drawn to her shapely legs. Miraculously, none of the mixture missed. In a distracted manner, he threw pieces of sliced cheddar into the pan to melt with the eggs.

Andrea flipped open a pair of baggy gray sweats she'd had folded under her arm with a disbelieving defensive gesture. In an uncomfortable tone of voice, she muttered while stepping into the elastic-legged drawstring-waist pants, "Look fast, then, ye of little vision, because it's all going back under lock and key, even as we speak."

Chagrined, Greg turned back to the stove, watching while he stirred the eggs. So far, he had avoided slobbering over the stove top, but it had been more through blind luck than any skill on his part. "Where do you work, anyhow? I can't see anybody letting you show up in that outfit. Do you run and change when you get there? Is that why you leave so early in the morning?"

"Actually, I teach an early-morning aerobics class geared for working people from six-thirty until seven-thirty. It gives them time to exercise, shower, change and still get to work on time. I do shower and change myself, but only into clean sweats." Greg groaned at that and Andrea looked smug. "Then I head for Washburne Junior High where I teach physical education for the remainder of the day." She glanced at her wrist, to the slim gold watch with its utilitarian brown leather strap. "And I'm running late, what with all the unusually scintillating conversation this morning. I'll have a quick glass of juice and be off." She reached for one of the two glasses of orange juice he had set on the table.

"Absolutely not." Quickly he held the tumbler to the table with his own hand, countermanding her efforts. "You can't possibly do all that physical work without a decent breakfast. By the time you find your shoes and get them on, this will be ready." With a flick of his spatula he indicated the skillet of eggs already nicely thickening.

"Damn, I'm really running late, and I don't know where I left them. I spend half my life looking for my shoes. If it's not them, then it's my car keys. I don't suppose you know..."

"I believe I landed on them when you knocked me off the couch this morning. You must have kicked them off before you fell asleep." He eyed her reflectively as she breathed a sigh of relief. "There's an old saying, something to the effect of 'a place for everything, and everything in its place' that might go a long way toward easing your frustrations."

"You must meet my mother sometime. She'd love you," Andrea muttered under her breath as she turned to retrieve the shoes from the living room.

"Sounds like a worthy woman of good taste and refinement," Greg returned blandly. "Too bad she's already spoken for."

Andrea gave him a meaningful glare over her shoulder, allowing it to speak for her.

Chapter Five

The ensuing week, however chaotically begun, went remarkably smoothly. The house's odd mixture of cramped occupants fell into a schedule of sorts, albeit not a totally smooth-running one. Andrea and Greg alternated nights between the bed in her room and the living-room couch. Somehow, even from the opposite end of the house, Greg was aware the second Andrea rose and would appear in the kitchen to breakfast with her, determined to add something edible to the morning fare. He would drink her health juice if she would at least sit with him if not join him in eating "normal" breakfast food. It was a quiet time in the house, a time of peace and tranquillity when they could get to know each other before the day's craziness had put them on edge. Andrea grew to look forward to it in an odd sort of way, even stooping to rummaging loudly through the cabinets the one morning he was late. And still she wouldn't admit that she was having an odd reaction to the absence of a person she professed not to like very much.

The boiler was replaced. Andrea paid for it with funds collected as tuition for the next semester's aerobics classes. Every time she walked into the kitchen, she thought about how that money could have bought new cabinets and hated the old ones even more.

Greg divided his days among apartment hunting with Karen, naps, and helping ready the upper apartment for its imminent occupancy. His naps grew shorter and further between. He accomplished a great deal on the second-floor flat, but he and Karen never did find an acceptable apartment. His jaundice faded noticeably, with each passing day and increasingly, Andrea found his presence more disturbing to her strangely off-balance mental state.

Andrea returned each evening around four-thirty after teaching school all day to shower and begin supper. Greg was oddly silent about some of the methods she used to achieve the end product—dinner on the table.

Monday night it was chicken tetrazzini. Greg gravely thanked her for using regular sliced mushrooms and not button as these were at least big enough to see easily and remove. She said she'd had him in mind when she'd bought them. Her thoughtfulness was reciprocated with a compliment on the high quality of the tetrazzini sauce the chicken resided in. She bit her lip and looked a little uncertainly in Karen's direction before responding that it was two cans of cream of chicken soup and a pint of sour cream and then bowed her head to examine an oddly shaped noodle on her plate.

She looked up again, surprised when nothing more than a noncommittal "Oh, well, it's very good" was forthcoming. Her look turned to shock when she saw the forkful of tetrazzini with a very large, very identifiable mushroom chunk halfway to his mouth. He noticed the look and in a slightly defensive tone informed her, "So maybe they'll grow on me."

Closing her mouth and willfully commanding her lips to smile, she only remarked, "I'm glad, I do tend to use them a lot when I cook."

God, they were being so polite to one another. She felt more strained and uncomfortable than she had when he was letting her have it. She suspected he had only eaten the damn mushroom to make up for having put her on the spot for the sauce recipe. What she couldn't figure out was why he felt it necessary to make amends at all. She had to keep reminding herself this was all a show for Karen, but it was tough going because the attraction felt more and more real.

They had taken to eating at the table in the living room as a way of unwinding after the pressures of the day. Tonight, the low glow of the burning fat-bodied candles not only was reflected by the blue-black depths of her hair, but also helped mask her unease as she fidgeted with the roughly woven cloth napkin on her lap. Desperately she cast around the recesses of her mind for a way to break the polite impasse and put things back on a normal footing; then she disparaged of her sanity for even wanting to.

After dinner, Karen and Tim disappeared suspiciously, leaving Greg and a decidedly awkward-feeling Andrea sitting on the sofa. She perched on its edge and felt sixteen again. Karen and Tim seemed determined to play the scheming parents out to find a match for their recalcitrant old-maid daughter. They had only forgotten their "We'll leave you young folks alone now, we know you don't want us old fogies around" exit line, and she rather suspected that had only been an oversight.

Greg lounged negligently back into the sofa cushions, looking totally comfortable and at ease. His legs were casually crossed, and his arms stretched back to encompass the long lines of the sofa back. He didn't seem to feel the slightest bit awkward over their being so obviously thrown together, she thought resentfully. In fact he seemed to be actually enjoying the situation. She stifled the urge to smack him.

Her suspicions were confirmed as she watched him taking in her poorly concealed squirming with the superior attitude one would expect of a physician who had identified some teeming colony on his microscope slide and knew the precise antidote to bring it under his control. His foot gently beat the air as he spoke. "What those two don't understand is that all of this obvious maneuvering is unnecessary. I may be slow on the pickup, but I'm not stupid. Living with you the past few days, I've come to realize that you're special. I'd be a fool to let you go simply to prove to Karen that she can't manage my life for me. I dropped empty acts of rebellion when I left my teens."

Time for a hasty exit, Andrea realized. This was getting to be a little heavy. Even if he was the most handsome man to cross her path that she could recall, he needed a nursemaid, not a wife. That inexplicable something vibrating between them could just inflict itself on some other lovelorn twosome. Long ago she had learned the odds against marriage. Now her acquired distaste for the matrimonial state had her labeling him a hypochondriacal wimp. He wasn't, of course—not really. And she knew it, but she was grasping at straws. Disparaging him was a last-ditch protective effort to shore up the widening breach in her defenses.

Nervously, she rose to her feet. "Yes, well," she began, hating the slight tremor in her voice, "I've spent so much time on the upstairs apartment that I really must devote some time down here. I think I'll try to strip some of the paint off the dining-room French doors. If you'll excuse me..." Her voice trailed off weakly.

Greg groaned and grimaced. "I have spent hours upstairs today painting and hanging kitchen cabinets. I was hoping maybe we could drive down to the lakefront and watch the whale fights."

Andrea was too late to prevent the escaping laugh. "I haven't heard that line since I was back in high school."

"Actually, that's about the last time I used it. I've been rather too busy since then to keep up with the latest expressions used to put the move on a good-looking woman."

"Sorry, but whether or not you've been through a long dry spell, I really do have to accomplish some work around here. I can't stand that bilious green in the dining room much longer." That was another problem with doctors. They led such directed, narrow lives. Imagine not even dating seriously for that length of time. Doctors spent so much energy immersed in their specializations that there was no room left for depth in any other aspects of their lives. They were shallow.

On the other hand, Andrea knew she was conveniently forgetting her own lack of depth in forming serious relationships, and she had also overlooked the total competence Greg had displayed in doing the handiwork around the house. He couldn't be *that* narrow and accomplish what he had.

Greg stood with a lithe movement that belied his physical condition. His arms were flung over his head in an unaffected stretching motion, and Andrea was utterly appalled by the sudden dryness in her mouth and the abrupt rise in her pulse rate.

His yawn stopped midstretch as he noticed her fascination. Either she had a very readable face, or else he had taken a rotation through psychiatry that gave him uncanny insight. "You can fight it as much as you want, Andrea. But there is something special between us," he said, "a definite magnetism flowing around us and working on us. We have to decide if it's going to be the undeniable attraction of North-South poles or the unfightable repulsion occurring between like poles. I choose going with the flow and not wasting energy trying to twist it into its opposite. It seems to me that would be an exhausting, and in the end, useless exercise in frustration." He crossed the room and slid an arm around her shoulders, gently walking her from the room. "Now, if you're quite sure you wouldn't care to reconsider my former suggestion, I guess after taking two naps today, I can manage to scrape up enough energy to spackle the cracks in the wall while you strip the woodwork."

Andrea latched on to his last offer as a line to safer topics and feelings. Greg gave her a knowing glance when she ignored the entire first part of his lecture and commented "You know before you can spackle, you'll have to first score the crack into an inverted V so that it's wider in the back than on the surface. That way the spackle won't pop..."

"I know how to plaster, Andrea," Greg interrupted imperturbably. "I grew up in an old farmhouse and my parents were absolute sticklers on renovating the proper way." He patted her shoulder. "You just change your clothes and take care of the stripping. Now there's a job I hate. I'll handle the walls, and I promise you won't regret a thing come the light of day."

Andrea rubbed the tip of her nose and squinted at him. "Sorry. It's the teacher in me. I don't mean to be insulting."

"Don't worry about it," Greg advised. Then he sighed as he picked up a a plastering spatula and tested its weight, muttering contemplatively, "I wonder if this is what Karen and Tim had in mind when they deserted us to a romantic evening together."

Andrea laughed. "It seems Karen doesn't know me all that well yet. If she had bothered to consult Tim, I'm sure he would have suspected as much. I guess I'm not the candle-and-moonlight type."

"Romance is an acquired taste. We'll take it slow. Start with a kiss or two in the plaster dust and work our way right up to hugging behind the paint-can stack. You'll love it. Especially with the terrific teacher you've got. I've made the study of women my lifework."

"In and out of school?"

"Hey, I was a devotee of the gentler sex long before I was a devotee of medicine. I broke my buns becoming captain of the high-school football team so I could impress this one little cheerleader."

Andrea paused, intrigued. "Did it work?"

He grimaced. "Yeah, but she turned out to have nothing going for her but a mean cartwheel and the best split I've ever seen. That's when I learned to check a little deeper than the surface for beauty." He looked directly at her.

Andrea sat on the ladder steps, deciding to ignore his last remark and find out what she could. "Where'd you go to high school? Karen's mom is living in Winnetka, a few miles away. That's definitely not farming country."

Greg was surprised. "You thought I grew up someplace like Winnetka? Heck, no. Too rich for our blood. Loretta married money. We didn't have it as kids. We grew up in Pennsylvania, out in the country. Dad had a nice little farm. We were comfortable, never lacked for anything important, but by no stretch of the imagination were we rich."

"So you went to high school there?"

"Yep, followed by Penn State and Johns Hopkins."

"Were you happy?" Andrea was genuinely interested now.

"Oh, yes. You won't believe it, but I never drew a serious breath until my senior year of high school. I had a ball. I got good grades mainly because the teachers all liked me, not because of any real effort on my part. And the girls fell all over themselves to get to the football players. Yes, I had a good time. Mom and Dad doted on me. I was an only child, for all practical purposes. Loretta was so much older she was gone by the time I was six. When my folks died in my senior year I had to do a lot of growing very fast. I had only myself to rely on for my future, and I knuckled down."

She hadn't meant to bring up sad memories. She stood and winked. "Yeah? And what about all those collegiate women and young nurses at Hopkins?"

"Well..." He made a deprecatory gesture.

Chuckling, she left to put on her grubbies.

* * *

The next day, Tuesday, found Greg wandering downstairs after a frustrating few hours spent trying to help Tim connect the upstairs kitchen appliances. They had worked in tight, cramped quarters the whole while and neither was in a very jolly mood. Tim entered the kitchen first and tried to head off an explosion by blocking Greg's view, but it was useless. Greg saw the way Andrea was making scalloped potatoes to go with dinner's main course of honey-glazed ham. She was using canned cheddar-cheese soup. Andrea tensed when Greg took the can in his hand and studied it. She had intended to have the casserole in the oven and the soup can buried deep in the garbage when they came down, but hadn't quite made it.

Greg was thunder in a cloud thick with electrical charges that was rapidly losing control over its occupant bolts. Sooner or later, the tensions in the house were bound to get to him and he would let fly, zapping Andrea with his sarcasm about her dependency on the bounty of canned-soup companies as he had the first two days. Her nerves frayed further as she realized this wasn't the time. He walked by with a noncommittal "Hmm, looks good" as he finished inspecting the proceedings on his way to the bath for a quick shower. "I'm starved."

Andrea dropped the handful of potatoes she had been carefully layering and simply stared after him. No suggestions to look into the savings of buying soup by the case? No queries as to the presence of mushrooms in the sauce? She decided he was just gathering his strength to lower the final boom with as much effect as possible. He was waiting for her to be off her guard. Well, he wouldn't get away with it. She wouldn't be frightened off, and she wouldn't change her cooking style either. There wasn't time after working all day to grate all that cheese and make the dumb stuff from scratch if they wanted to eat at a decent hour. And it tasted the same anyway. She simply would not apologize for her cooking. It was good. Unorthodox perhaps, but good.

At the end of the evening, Andrea was alarmed to discover that when not eye to eye over a can of soup or a mushroom, it was very easy to fall into an effortless camaraderie with Greg. Typically, people involved in distasteful remodeling work found their nerves on edge and their tongues quick to go for the jugular of anyone within sarcasm distance. They had spent the evening with the nauseating odors of sealant and paint remover, forcing them to open windows, which alleviated the smell but left them to freeze while working. Things should have been strained. She should have been consistently biting her tongue to hold back the verbal abuse she normally threw around under such conditions, but she hadn't. Instead, Greg had tuned the radio in on an oldies program. The evening had been spent singing along with the Four Tops and the Four Seasons, occasionally demonstrating a nostalgic dance step from high-school sock hops past.

He really was fun to be with, Andrea realized ruefully as they munched their way through a bowl of hot popcorn buttered with real butter and celebrated a final adieu to the awful green dining-room wall.

She thought she had cleverly evaded his good-night kiss and whatever other moves he had intended to bring into play. But she must have been less subtle than she thought because Greg had laughed and said, "Run if you want to, Andrea. You can't get far in this little house. Time is on my side. Along with both of the house's other occupants, I might add. You haven't got a chance, but the chase will make it more interesting." He kissed her on the tip of the nose despite her evasive tactics. "Go to bed," he instructed. "I'll see you in the morning."

Andrea closed the door on his grin and brushed her teeth with a vengeance born of desperation. It simply wasn't fair. Here she was, odd man out in her own home. There had been an uprising and the tenants had taken over the landlord's premises. How had she missed the coup?

She was running scared.

* * *

Wednesday evening found everyone grossly overtired. The men had spent the day lugging furniture up to the efficiency apartment, retrieving Karen and Tim's boxes of stored household items from the basement and trying to set up a semblance of a living arrangement. That project would take days to complete, but enough was accomplished to warrant a christening celebration and the inception of a genuine residency in the upper apartment.

Andrea was tired as well. She had run her morning aerobics class. Then the junior high's teachers had complained about the students' general rambunctiousness, no doubt due to the cold snap currently sitting over Chicago and the students sudden indoor confinement. She had really put them through their paces in an effort to bring their energy levels down to a manageable level. The crowning blow had come with a phone call from the Chandler Leisure Center, whose late-afternoon class was instructorless due to a flu bug. That last unexpected aerobics class had been sheer torture.

At least Karen had thought to make a salad and start a gelatin mold to set. But Andrea didn't even think twice about opening a can of not just any soup, but cream of mushroom soup, to throw together an easy tuna casserole. She was too exhausted to even contemplate anything more complicated.

Karen bounced into the kitchen, as much as was humanly possible for a pregnant woman to bounce, and announced, "We need to celebrate the inauguration of the upstairs apartment. I'm going to bake a cake. What kind of exotic recipes have you got floating around?"

Andrea was not so tired that she didn't realize the implication of her next move. If the thunderbolts finally zapped, so be it. She reached into the cabinets to withdraw a can of tomato soup. After handing it to a bemused Karen, she took a great deal of perverse pleasure in looking up her recipe for tomato-soup cake.

Karen almost gagged. "Are you sure about this?" she asked with one hand over her mouth and eyes wide.

"It tastes just like a spice cake, which I don't have the ingredients for. Use the tube pan, and I'll make some penuche frosting. It's really good. I love it. So will you."

"Well... if you're really sure..."

"Trust me. You'll like it." If nothing else could serve to force Greg to show his true colors again, this would. Andrea suspected he would prefer an agonizing death, asphyxiated from sealant vapors, than to eating tomato-soup cake.

But she was wrong. They sat on the floor, surrounding a pile of chunky rainbow-hued burning candles. Karen leaned back, groaning as she patted her burgeoning stomach. "I really must find out from the doctor what kind of exercises I can do while I'm pregnant. Now that I'm feeling well again, I can literally feel my muscles turning into limp spaghetti. If I don't start moving now, I'll never get back into shape when this is all over."

Plainly horrified, Andrea looked up from gathering a fingerful of frosting from where it had dripped onto the cakeplate. "Over my dead body. I've said it before, that kid is only half-baked. You'll put yourself into premature labor and lose it for sure."

Greg seemed about to speak, but Karen cut him off. "All I know is that if I've reached the point in this pregnancy where cake made from tomato soup tastes good, then pickles and ice cream at midnight must be next. I'll be a two-ton Tess long before the baby comes if I lie around the way you two seem to require." She cast an accusatory glance encompassing both Andrea and Tim.

Greg glanced down at the fluted white paper plate in front of him, empty except for a few crumbs. He seemed to be caught in some internal struggle, but whatever it was passed quickly. Calm again, he reached for the serrated knife they had been using on the cake and sliced himself his third decent-size serving. He looked meaningfully into Andrea's flashing blue eyes while taking a large bite.

He was only eating it to annoy her, she knew. She was irritated that his calm acceptance of her planned dig made her feel small and childish for instigating the plan. "You're not fooling me for one second, Mr. Hotshot Doctor. Your repressed taste buds are shrieking their revulsion and committing suicide by the dozen while you sit there pretending to be calm. I can hear their cries of agony all the way over here. You're trying to break me, and you won't get away with it, do you hear me? I will not fall in love with a food fussbudget. I will not allow it. I won't!"

Two pairs of eyes swung to catch Greg's reaction to this unwarranted outburst. Tim looked especially interested. He had grown up next door to Andrea. In all those years, she had never displayed the temperamental side of her nature to anywhere near the extent she had shown it since Greg's arrival five days ago.

"Is that what you're doing, Andrea?" Greg asked in polite, interested tones. "Falling in love?"

"No!" she denied, now almost yelling in her horror at her own condemning words. "I could never fall in love with someone who falls apart over the ingredients in a lousy cake!"

Greg watched Andrea's face redden with the heat of her words. According to Karen, Andrea was always calm, nothing seemed to faze her. She'd even faced Karen and Tim's problems with an optimistic logic, not even acknowledging that everyone else had given up, merely wringing their hands and gnashing their teeth. Now here she was, downright irrational. How long would it be before she realized that it had not been Greg falling apart over the cake's ingredients, but rather Andrea herself?

"We'll come back to this interesting topic another time," he promised, his eyes gleaming. "When we're alone. Right now I think it would be more productive to get back to Karen's concern over exercising." He turned his attention to his niece, infuriating Andrea further with his easy dismissal of her display of temper. She was itching for a fight and it had been denied her, producing a feeling quite foreign to her normal good nature.

"Now there are many exercises that are perfectly all right for a pregnant woman. In fact, if you look around, I'm sure you'll be able to find a prenatal exercise class. That way, you won't have to worry about every little thing you try. Those classes are carefully designed to eliminate any potentially harmful movements. I believe I said it before: if you're physically fit, chances are good you'll have an easier delivery and quicker recovery. I always recommend some type of physical activity to my patients, even it it's only a brisk walk."

One of the candles hissed as it drowned in a puddle of its own wax, and Tim looked doubtful. "Are you sure about this, Greg? She was so sick..."

"Naturally I don't know all the details, and she should check with her own doctor before she does anything. But if it was simple morning sickness, no bleeding or anything, there's no medical reason why she shouldn't do gentle exercises. I'm not suggesting she go in for Olympic training."

Andrea was trying to settle down, having realized at last that she was the only one out of control. It was all to no avail as Greg once more turned to include her in the conversation.

"Now there's a class you might consider offering, Andrea. I could help you in deciding a program of appropriate exercises, and you'd make a lot of expectant mothers happy." He waited patiently for her reaction.

Andrea looked at him as though he had just sprouted a second head. "Are you out of your mind? Pregnant women make me crazy. I want to encase them in Saran wrap and put them on a shelf for nine months, not worry myself sick lest I cause one of them to miscarry."

"You must get over this archaic notion that pregnant women can crack and break like an egg. In many ways a woman's body is functioning at its peak during a pregnancy. What are you going to do when you find yourself having a baby? Go to bed and set a timer for nine months? You may as well get over your fear now, because sooner or later it's going to happen to you, and you won't be able to put your head under a pillow and hide for the duration." Greg's impatient gaze pinned her.

"There is no reason for me to get over my fears, either now or later. I doubt if I'll ever have children."

Greg's gaze sharpened even further. "What do you mean? Is there something I don't know about? Are you unable to have children for some reason?"

The hardness of his tone surprised the other three, and made the question an important one.

"Physically I wouldn't know, as I've never been in the position to find out. But I do know that emotionally I couldn't handle it. I'll never have children."

Tim sat back, sighing and shaking his head.

"I don't understand," Greg probed disbelievingly. "You love children. What the hell—you even have a Brownie troop. Nobody but a bona fide kid-lover would take that on if they didn't have to. Look at the time you spent working on that Pinewood Derby car for the kid next door. Don't try to tell me you don't like children."

"Of course I like children," Andrea interrupted impatiently. "I never said I didn't."

"Then what exactly did you say? What is the problem?"

Andrea's voice rose. "There is no problem! Any problem was taken care of when I decided not to have children! Now if I were to get pregnant, then there'd be a problem!"

Greg leaned forward to emphasize his next statement. One hand supported his tilting posture while the other pointed at his chest. "Andrea, *I* want to have children."

Now Andrea leaned forward. They were virtually nose to nose. "Bully for you. I am not stopping you."

"Evidently, you are." Karen and Tim might as well have been invisible for all the attention they received. Andrea resented the patient forbearance in his tone as Greg explained what he saw as the simple facts of life to her. It smacked of condescension. "Perhaps I have not made myself adequately clear the past few days. *You* are the one I plan to have carry my children—a fact that will require one or more nine-month pregnancies on your part. Therefore, unless you want to spend a large portion of the next few years in bed, which would be unhealthy for you and my unborn children and which I would never allow anyway, you had better address yourself to overcoming these fears, nameless as they seem to be."

Karen's peripheral debate with Tim over whether the calories in a second piece of cake would be worth it or not had stopped. Now her head whipped back and forth between the two conversants with the speed and agility of a Ping-Pong ball in a championship tournament. Her amazed look said as clearly as any words that when she had set the ball in motion a few days back, she had never anticipated this fast a response.

"There is no way in hell," Andrea began forcefully, less than an inch from Greg's nose, "that I will ever carry your baby or babies. So you can just pack your...whatever back in your old kit bag and find somebody else to dump this on. I'm not interested. Not now, not ever."

"Give me one good reason why not." Greg knew Andrea was not indifferent to him. He knew half of her ill humor was a camouflage, an effort to deny the attraction between them. He saw through it. He had assumed she was equally aware of the reason behind her feistiness. Maybe she hadn't reached that point of awareness yet.

"I have no intention of discussing this any further. We are supposed to be celebrating the completion of Karen and Tim's apartment. I hardly call arguing with you much of a celebration. As a matter of fact, I would consider it rather dampening."

"Fine. We'll discuss it tomorrow."

"No, we will not. It is none of your business. Furthermore, tomorrow is a free day, and I intend to spend it in Lombard at Kohler's Trading Post checking out the secondhand furniture."

"I'll go with you."

"I don't think so. This is one of my favorite leisure-time activities. I don't want it ruined with a lot of badgering."

"Okay, I promise I won't badger you," Greg gruffly pledged. "Just let me come, and I'll behave."

Andrea shot him a disbelieving glance. "Your fingers are probably crossed behind your back," she accused.

"Scout's honor," Greg swore solemnly, displaying three fingers raised in imitation of the Scout pledge sign.

"Oh, all right, but if you start in on me, I'll leave you stranded in Lombard, and that's a promise, not an idle threat." She turned to glare at Karen and complained, "This is all your fault!"

Karen gasped at the unfair recrimination. Her hand went to her chest in a dramatic gesture. "My fault? I had nothing to do with this, other than wanting you to meet my only living relative outside of my parents," she said in wounded tones. "It was a great honor I paid you. Shows how highly I think of you."

"Oh, spare me. Why couldn't you have introduced me to some senile doting aunt or a harmless old uncle with a beer belly?"

"Probably because I don't have either one. It's him or nothing, I'm afraid," Karen pointed out reasonably.

"Aachhh, I give up." She glared at Tim, and it was his turn to come under fire. "Why'd you have to marry somebody with such weird relatives? Couldn't you have been a little more selective?"

Tim was clearly wounded. "Hey! Don't blame me. Haven't you ever heard that love is blind? It's not my fault I fell for her, hook, line and sinker. I was bedazzled by her seductive charms and roped up to the altar before I even knew what I was doing." He pulled his wife over and began planting wet kisses in all the ticklish spots up and down the side of her neck. "She was so romantic and wily," he protested while Karen giggled helplessly. "Such a woman of the world, I couldn't help myself."

Andrea threw up her hands in disgust and rose to gather up the paper plates. "That does it, now they're getting mushy on me. I'm leaving before I gag. Dr. Greg here can take notes. It's been a long time between women. He told me so himself. Probably needs a refresher course."

"Perhaps you'd like to give me the opportunity to demonstrate my abilities of total recall." Greg had his own temper back under control and was grinning up at her.

"No, thanks," Andrea said. "I've had about all I can handle for one evening. I'm going to see if Lisa can't be more gracious company." She started toward the stairs, suddenly needing to talk to her best friend and Tim's twin.

"Say hi for me," Tim instructed.

"Will do," Andrea absently agreed, intent on not tripping down the stairs.

Tim's attention turned to his wife's only living relative other than her parents. "You don't seem too upset by all this."

"It'll just take longer, that's all." Greg sighed as he stretched his arms high over his head. "She's a tougher nut to crack than I first thought. But she'll crack, never you fear. In the meantime, it would be nice to know a little more about what I'm up against. I couldn't figure out why a woman like her wasn't snatched up long ago, but I'm beginning to see. I'll bet the men around here aren't as blind as I thought, but have simply been shut out by Andrea."

"Possibly so," Tim agreed thoughtfully. "She certainly hasn't dated much since we've been here."

Karen nodded her head in agreement. "Lots of male friends, but strictly friends, if you know what I mean."

"Do you know what it's all about?" Greg questioned Tim directly, since he'd known Andrea the longest.

"I might have some ideas," Tim admitted reluctantly. "But I think the answers should come from Andrea. It's not my place to spill her secrets."

Chapter Six

Andrea paced the short length of Lisa's apartment living room, made an almost military about-face at the far wall and returned to stand in front of the chair where her friend sat. Every word Andrea spoke was punctuated with wide hand gestures and dramatic body language that showed a blatant disregard for the room's furnishings. The subdued light escaping from the pink tiffany lamp shade lent an even ruddier hue to Andrea's flushed complexion as she flung rash comments and rhetorical questions, one terse word after another across the room. "I tell you, Lisa, I'm being driven out of my own home. A stranger in my own land."

"Come now, surely you're overreacting. How can he have such a strong effect on you if you truly feel nothing?" Lisa imperturbably flicked a wide-tooth comb through her wheat-colored bob. "If he really left you cold, you'd be able to ignore him, just like every other man you've bumped into since hitting puberty."

"It's not that easy," Andrea assured her. "This time, the man's a permanent fixture on the premises. Believe me, it's a lot harder to ignore. Besides, this one would get under anybody's skin."

The tilt of Lisa's head combined with the expression on her peach-tinted lips clearly spelled her disbelief.

The look acted as a pinprick to Andrea's self-righteous balloon, and it suddenly deflated, leaving her to fold dejectedly into a casually upholstered tan corduroy armchair, staring at her naked fingernails, each one propped against its opposite in a thoughtful pose. "I ought to buy myself some fingernail polish," she interposed morosely. "It's time I started taking care of myself. Mother's right. The clean, well-scrubbed look is all right for little girls with pigtails, but a woman should cultivate her looks a little. Even Greg insinuated I could use a little cosmetic aid."

"Do you hear what you're saying?" Lisa demanded. "Now I know this is serious. Tell me everything, but this time in some kind of coherent order."

Under Lisa's direction, Andrea began. "It's been awful. Since the moment I opened the front door to him a few days ago, I haven't been myself. Jumping all over everybody at the least provocation. Perfectly awful," she repeated for lack of a better adjective.

Lisa moved impatiently and Andrea tried again. "From the time he first rang the doorbell, we've been at each other's throats. And it's not that he's a dog and I'm being a snob or anything. If anything, he's every red-blooded woman's American dream, at least on the surface," she admitted.

"So what's the problem then?"

"He's a jerk." Andrea stated it empirically, albeit with a regretful sigh. "Not only that, he's a wimp as well."

Lisa sounded as though she were strangling and Andrea looked concerned until she realized her friend was really struggling against laughter. "A jerk and a wimp, huh? Quite a damning combination. You won't mind if I ask you to elaborate a tad, will you?"

Andrea had no objections. She had come to talk it out, hadn't she? "In the first place," she began with dark enthusiasm, "he hates mushrooms and I might as well employ Chinese water torture as serve him anything with canned soup as an ingredient. The maturity of his attitude lags a *minimum* of twenty-five years behind the rest of his body." Here she blushed as she thought of the rest of his body and paused in her narrative to see what effect her dire accusations were having. Lisa didn't seem overly affected one way or the other, so she plowed on, determined to recruit at least one person to her own camp.

"He has no stamina or physical reserves whatsoever. Eight weeks ago he caught hepatitis. Eight weeks! And he's still taking naps and can't seem to get his strength back. Karen thinks we ought to get married so he has someone to bond with and that will make him recover faster. Can you believe it? Who am I, Florence Nightingale? Haven't I got enough aches and pains of my own without marrying into a whole fresh supply?" The questions were increasingly rhetorical, as Andrea gave Lisa no time to respond.

"His life has been so closely directed for so long, he's lost sight of anything other than doctoring. And not only is he a doctor, but he's an obstetrician! We'd never have any alone time, although he swears he's going to concentrate on broadening his horizons now. How can he? He'll always be getting called into the hospital. And worst of all—" this last came with a certain touch of relish "—he's fiscally irresponsible, just like my dad." She sat back in the chair, well pleased with her presentation and its irrefutable logic.

"My, you certainly have covered all bases, haven't you?" Lisa responded with a gentle smile. She set the comb down and began to use both hands to tick off Andrea's complaints. "Let's see if I have this right. His taste in food is a little conservative, he's slowly recovering from a debilitating illness, and he's intelligent and hardworking enough that you feel secure he'll be successful in his chosen field. The only thing I'm not clear on is the fiscal irresponsibility

SILHOUETTE

♥ **PRESENTS** ♥

A Real Sweetheart of a Deal!

7 FREE GIFTS

PEEL BACK THIS CARD AND SEE
WHAT YOU CAN GET! THEN...

Complete the Hand Inside

It's easy! To play your cards right, just match this card with the cards inside.

Turn over for more details...

Incredible isn't it? Deal yourself in <u>right now</u> and get 7 fabulous gifts.
ABSOLUTELY FREE.

1. 4 BRAND NEW SILHOUETTE ROMANCE® NOVELS— FREE!
Sit back and enjoy the excitement, romance and thrills of four fantastic novels. You'll receive them as part of this winning streak!

2. A BEAUTIFUL AND PRACTICAL PEN AND WATCH – FREE!
This watch with its leather strap and digital read-out certainly looks elegant – but it is also extremely practical. Its quartz crystal movement keeps precision time! And the pen with its slim good looks will make writing a pleasure.

3. AN EXCITING MYSTERY BONUS – FREE!
And still your luck holds! You'll also receive a special mystery bonus. You'll be thrilled with this surprise gift. It will be the source of many compliments as well as a useful and attractive addition to your home.

PLUS

THERE'S MORE. THE DECK IS STACKED IN YOUR FAVOR. HERE ARE THREE MORE WINNING POINTS. YOU'LL ALSO RECEIVE:

4. A MONTHLY NEWSLETTER – FREE!
It's "Heart to Heart" – the insider's privileged look at our most popular writers, upcoming books and even recipes from your favorite authors.

5. CONVENIENT HOME DELIVERY
Imagine how you'll enjoy having the chance to preview the romantic adventures of our Silhouette heroines in the convenience of your own home! Here's how it works. Every month we'll deliver 6 new books right to your door. There's no obligation, and if you decide to keep them, they'll be yours for only $1.95. And there's no extra charge for postage and handling.

6. MORE GIFTS FROM TIME TO TIME – FREE!
It's easy to see why you have the winning hand. In addition to all the other special deals available only to our home subscribers, you can look forward to additional free gifts throughout the year.

SO DEAL YOURSELF IN – YOU CAN'T HELP BUT WIN!

You'll Fall In Love With This Sweetheart Deal From Silhouette!

SILHOUETTE BOOKS
FREE OFFER CARD

4 FREE BOOKS • DIGITAL WATCH AND MATCHING PEN • FREE MYSTERY BONUS • INSIDER'S NEWSLETTER • HOME DELIVERY • MORE SURPRISE GIFTS

☐ *YES! Deal me in. Please send me four free Silhouette Romance novels, the pen and watch and my **free mystery gift** as explained on the opposite page.*

215 CIL HAXM

First Name	Last Name

PLEASE PRINT

Address	Apt.

City	State

Zip Code

Offer limited to one per household and not valid for present subscribers. Prices subject to change.

SILHOUETTE NO RISK GUARANTEE

- There is no obligation to buy – the free books and gifts remain yours to keep.
- You receive books before they're available in stores.
- You may end your subscription at any time – just let us know.

PRINTED IN U.S.A.

Remember! To win this hand, all you have to do is place your sticker inside and DETACH AND MAIL THE CARD BELOW. You'll get four free books, a free pen and watch and a mystery bonus.
BUT DON'T DELAY! MAIL US YOUR LUCKY CARD TODAY!

If card has been removed write to:
Silhouette, 901 Fuhrmann Blvd., P.O. Box 1867, Buffalo, N.Y. 14269-1867

BUSINESS REPLY CARD

First Class   Permit No. 717   Buffalo, NY

Postage will be paid by addressee

Silhouette Books
901 Fuhrmann Blvd.
P.O. Box 1867
Buffalo, N.Y.
14240-9952

NO POSTAGE
NECESSARY
IF MAILED
IN THE
UNITED STATES

part." She raised an expectant eyebrow, evidently waiting for Andrea to elaborate.

Andrea wore a slightly disconcerted expression. She could have coped with the first three, she told herself grimly. But the money, now that was enough all by itself. She raised her head to tell Lisa so. She had her on that one. "Karen says he went through medical school on loans. That means he has to be thousands of dollars in debt. You know how I feel about getting involved with anyone like that."

"If this is the best you can come up with, love, you really are grasping at straws."

Andrea gasped her indignation. "What do you mean?"

"What I'm saying," she said with a kind smile, the type used in explaining the facts of life to an idiot, "is that you and I both know that a lot of people don't like mushrooms. A lot of people put in long hours to establish their careers. Hepatitis is not in the same ballpark as hypochondria, and medical school is wildly expensive. Almost all doctors have to take out loans, *but they pay them back*. They're no more or less irresponsible than the rest of us poor slobs. Now," she continued in false solicitude, "why don't we try to get to the real heart of the matter? I find it odd that you've never bothered to manufacture excuses for avoiding a male before. I think you've never been interested enough to worry about the consequences."

Andrea thanked Lisa for lending an ear to her problems and returned home thoughtfully subdued. With the new boiler heating efficiently and Karen and Tim's back bedroom nicely vacated, there was no reason for Greg to sleep on the sofa. She missed seeing his dark head starkly juxtaposed against the cream sheets of the fold-out couch. The room seemed to lack life. In a reflective gesture, she rubbed her hand the length of a nubby pillow. Her hand clenched involuntarily, its fingernails digging into her palm. Resolutely, she forced it open, even as she forced her mind to accept the truth of much of what Lisa had said.

The roadblocks she had thrown up against Greg were petty, inconsequential half-truths. The crux of the problem lay within herself. His easy laugh and bantering manner as he worked on the dining room with her spoke of a sense of humor that would surely bloom with proper encouragement. His loans were probably within reason. Medical schools were expensive; not many could afford the tuition without floating a loan. In her heart she knew he was not the type to get in over his head. She was sure he had every expectation of paying them back. Yet, would she be able to overcome her fears regarding loans and money in general? She had watched her mother age years too early under the weight of her father's charm and wit. He too had been a doctor. And doctors were always good for a loan from the bank. But when this doctor didn't find doctoring "fulfilling" enough and went off to a low-paying research job after taking on school loans, mortgage payments and clinic equipment debts, then the banks weren't so thrilled. They got downright testy.

She had both loved and hated her father. And her childhood had scarred her. She was only just beginning to realize how deeply the scars ran. She had vowed to be self-sufficient, never relying on anyone else—the way her mother had her father, the way Tim had Karen. Where did it get you? Living on somebody else's charity. Could she relinquish that hard-won control to a second party at this point? The intellectual knowledge that Greg wasn't like her father, that he could balance desires and reality was still only an intellectual realization. It had yet to be internalized.

But Andrea continued to argue with herself. Even if she did internalize all her wonderful insights concerning the homeless M.D., wasn't it just a little *too* coincidental that he was trying to move in on the first female he saw right after emerging from medical school? How very convenient that just when he was ready to get on with his life Andrea suddenly seemed to embody his wifely wish list of attributes. Then again, it was also possible he was simply feeling sorry for her. He had to know by now that her backbone consisted of ninety-nine percent mush. Possibly he had twisted gratitude and sympathy into what he thought was love. Some morning he'd wake up and realize what he'd done, and bingo, he'd be gone. Think of all the good-looking women an all-female clientele doctor would see. If—and this was what Andrea really suspected—Greg was simply ready to settle down and anybody would do, he would be better advised to wait a bit. Someone better would surely come along. Meeting some strange schedule Greg had set up for his life was not a very good basis for marriage. And Andrea was determined to point that out to him at the earliest opportunity.

Schedule be darned! She wanted somebody who wanted *her*—not the fulfillment of some nebulous daydream of what married life between a high-school quarterback and an infatuated cheerleader would be. Andrea couldn't do a split to save her soul. She hadn't even made the first round of cuts at cheerleading tryouts. Maybe she should point out to him that unquestioning pom-pom waving was not her style.

Then there was Peggy. If he knew about Peggy, understood what had happened eleven years ago, he might stop pushing so hard and give her a little breathing space...time. What she ought to do was explain her point of view and maybe give him a chance to convince her of his sincerity.

Giving her head a decisive nod, she left the room to get ready for bed. Yes. Tomorrow. She'd stop hiding behind manufactured excuses. Mushrooms shouldn't be allowed to stand in the way of a chance at true love. They were only a fungus, after all. Nothing might come of it, but at least she wouldn't look back later, wistfully caught in what-could-have-beens. Her shoulders straightened resolutely. Armed with her toothbrush, she closeted herself in the bathroom.

Thursday dawned clear and bright. Unusual for Chicago's grayest month of the year. Andrea watched the faint early-morning light struggle through the kitchen windows.

There was something about clean windows, she mused. They maximized the light. Later in the day, when the sunlight came streaming in, the antiquated kitchen might appear almost quaint. But since the change from daylight saving time to standard three weeks ago, there hadn't been a whole lot of light at six in the morning, and one needed a certain amount of... imagination when viewing the unremodeled kitchen.

She looked up as Greg entered the room, humming a popular tune.

"Why are you dressed in sweats? Are you going running?" she asked.

"Nope," he replied laconically.

Andrea raised an eyebrow in silent question and Greg relented as he turned to light the flame under the teakettle.

"You agreed last night that I could spend the day with you. So I'm going to your exercise class with you."

"Uh, Greg, I don't really think that's a very good idea. Why don't you wait here until I'm done? Go for a quick mile run or something. We'll spend the rest of the day together. I promise."

Greg was evidently feeling stubborn this morning. His single "Nope" spoke volumes. "I won't be that out of place. Surely there must be a few men in your class. Even if they just come to ogle the instructor, I'll bet there are some."

"Three. But that's not the point. What I'm trying to say is that most of these people have been coming for months. I do sixty minutes of intensive stretching and aerobics. They all keep pace pretty well, and I've stopped taking it easy on them."

"I won't hold the class up, Andrea," Greg promised, dismissing her worries from over the top of his teacup and leaning back against the countertop.

"It's just that you shouldn't jump right into this. You've got to work your way back gradually. You've been sick, for crying out loud!"

Greg methodically refilled his teacup, paying strict attention to the task before raising his eyes to hers and responding, "I won't overdo. I'll stay in the back and stop if it gets to be too much. I can always sleep in the car on the way out to Lombard. It's a good hour's trip, isn't it?"

"You'll have a relapse! Why can't you be reasonable about this?" Andrea was beginning to sound distraught.

Greg gave a low roar, "For God's sake, Andrea. I'm a doctor. Stop the overprotective-mother routine and credit me with some intelligence. I know what I can and cannot do! Maybe you ought to stop and question why you're so concerned over me. It just might be a highly productive line of inquiry."

Andrea recoiled a step. Greg was right. She was overprotective and did worry too much. She'd make a lousy mother. She'd always be trying to smooth the kids' path, smothering them with her concern. If Greg wanted to have every muscle ache for the next few days, that was his problem. He was, after all, all grown-up. And he had asked a viable question. She turned the puzzle in her mind for an instant and gave up.

"Fine." She shrugged before gathering her reserves around her like a cloak. She looked at him carefully, noticing the jaundice had all but disappeared, leaving his mahogany orbs clear and bright. "Just tell me one thing: Are you doing this to prove a point?"

"No. I want to see what you do. I figure it'll give me one more key to the elusive Miss Andrea Conrades."

"Because if you are," she persisted, "it's a waste of time. I know you're not a wimp, and I'm sorry I called you one. You've done remarkably well, considering how sick you were. I only said those things about you because I was panicking. I'm attracted to you. You make me feel things I've never felt before. I'm not sure I want to feel them, either." Her eyes searched the room, unable to look directly at him while she made this admission. "Letting myself feel these things instead of fighting them . . . well, it's not as simple as it sounds. It means facing a lot of emotional issues I'm not sure I'm ready to face." Finally she looked directly at him. "But I'm going to try, Greg. I really am."

"That's all I'm asking. For both of us to make the effort. If it doesn't work out, it won't be from lack of trying." He kissed the top of her shiny hair in a light gesture and wrapped the lean length of a masculine arm around her waist. "Now, we'd better get moving. Those early-morning exercise fanatics await." And he guided her toward the front door.

By nine o'clock they had both showered, eaten a more filling breakfast than just the tea they had managed earlier and were back on the road. Andrea was driving because the exercise class had indeed been hard on Greg. He drifted into sleep, one hand cushioning the side of his head from the cold window. Taking in the long muscular body folded into the cramped seat next to hers, Andrea sent up a short prayer on a wry chuckle.

May he not regain his strength too quickly, she implored the heavens. Operating with only half his normal steam up, he was proving difficult enough to handle. She could only imagine the hardships involved in keeping up with the man beside her when it was full steam ahead.

She parked on the opposite side of Saint Charles Road from Kohler's Trading Post and gently shook Greg's shoulder. "Greg? We're here. Wake up."

It was amazing how easily he made the transition from sound sleep to alert wakefulness. That ability must be a medical-school entrance prerequisite. Without that particular skill, students would never make it through the long grind of internship and residency, she guessed. At any rate, he sat up immediately, passed a quick hand over his eyes and looked around expectantly. With no doubt as to where he was, he opened his door and circled to Andrea's side, courteously escorting her from the car.

Crossing the blacktopped street, they passed through the unlocked gates of the trading post. Greg stopped so suddenly that Andrea knocked up against him, a fact she didn't seem to mind in the least. She had made her decision to try to make things work and was now at peace with herself. After she steadied herself, her laughter rang out. She glanced up and caught the incredulous expression on Greg's face as he viewed the place.

She turned to look with him, trying to recapture the overwhelming sense of awe the trading post had inspired the first time she'd stepped through its gates. "It's really something, isn't it?" she questioned, absently flicking the rope of long hair the light wind had tossed in her face back over her shoulder.

Greg squinted in the bright morning light as he studied the seemingly endless rows of rusting refrigerators, old wringer washers, broken chairs, and shopping carts full of nameless gizmos. Surveying the chaotic scene with its casually parked trailers filled with church pews and school desks and the two low-lying buildings, he agreed. "I had no idea you were such a master in the art of understatement." He took one more look around before looking at her for the first time since entering the odd setting. "I'm surprised this is allowed within the city limits." Andrea laughed as he inquired further, "Have you ever actually bought anything here?"

"Well, I can see you're settling on the right side of town. You're a true North Shore snob already."

He pushed the hair back from her face for her, tunneling his hands under its heavy fall. "No, I'm serious. Have you ever bought anything here?"

"Absolutely," she assured him while rummaging in the depths of her shoulder bag. She placed the cloth-covered rubber band retrieved from its confines between her lips while she pulled her hair back with both hands. Speaking in muffled tones, she poked the air with an available elbow to indicate the surrounding area. "This is mostly for people looking for parts and pieces of things they need to repair something they already have. I did buy some of those for the house, though." She indicated a sorry-looking pile of storm windows and doors farther back on the lot. "Fit perfectly, too." She guided him toward the door of the first building after successfully wrapping the rubber band around her hair at the base of her neck in an off-kilter but effective George Washington ponytail. "But I must admit, most of the nice things I'm interested in are inside."

"I'll just bet," Greg muttered in a disbelieving tone.

"You don't really expect them to dump the good stuff out here to the mercy of the elements, do you? And let me remind you, you invited yourself along on this particular sojourn, so lighten up. I enjoy this place, so at least pretend to be having a good time, okay? Watch your—"

"Damn it anyway! You let your warning go a little late. Why the hell are those things hanging there?" Greg glared up at the tangled collections of ice skates hanging from the low rafters by the strength of their laces. The entire assemblage swayed from the force of his collision. "I damn near lost my head at the neckline!"

Andrea sighed. What had she been thinking of? This would never work. So what if he was the most devastatingly handsome man she had ever bumped into? So what if his look, not to mention his one kiss, sent her pulse racing and put her heart under as much strain as a ten-mile run? He'd had his head in his books too long. He was unsalvageable. Once the sexual highs had faded, she'd be stuck with a handsome, high IQ'd, boring stick-in-the-mud. Her foot tapped impatiently as she took in his irritated mien. No flair for fun. No spirit of adventure. She would curl up and die married to a man with no sense of humor. He may as well be a hundred years old.

Greg sensed Andrea's perturbation and pasted a sickly smile on his face, but he quickly gave up the struggle. "Give me a minute, honey," he pleaded. "My head hurts like hell. I'm sure it's an interesting place. Just...give me a minute."

She had to laugh. Her mood lightened. He was impossible, but he was trying...she'd settle for that. "Okay, but that's all you get, a minute." She started determinedly forward. "Now, as I was saying before you walked into those skates, watch your head. There are a lot of things displayed from the ceiling as well as in the aisles. So be careful."

"Thanks, I'll do that," he responded wryly, ducking a collection of outdated iron rug-beaters and other undefinable tools. He turned sideways, having to edge his way through a crowded aisle. "Are you sure this is safe? I've never seen so much stuff in one spot. It's got to be a fire hazard."

Andrea stopped to throw him a warning look over her shoulder. "Would you prefer to wait in the car while I browse?" she inquired acidly, both hands planted firmly on her hips as she stared at him.

He threw his hands up in a gesture of surrender, quick to placate her. "No, no. I am nothing if not a good sport."

She let an inelegant snort give her opinion of that and momentarily stopped by a table so full of romance novels that some had slid into a heap on the floor. She thought about thumbing through a few, but Greg's despairing "You wouldn't make me spend my day picking out junk books, would you?" made her move on. She could always come back later.

The aisle after the one with the twenty-five-hundred-dollar antiquated three-station barbershop innards displayed two massive pecan-finished corner cabinets jammed behind several other items. She stretched as far as she could and tipped her head sideways to read the scrawled chalk pricing: "Three hundred ninety-five dollars or both for six hundred and ninety-five dollars." Her head remained tilted while she considered it before turning to Greg. "That's probably fair, don't you think?"

Greg's hands were stuffed into his jeans back pockets while he rocked from heel to toe, studying the pieces.

"They're certainly good-looking," he allowed. "What did you have in mind for them?"

Andrea folded her arms across her midriff, a position her father had consistently disparaged as "hugging her buggy," and again returned her attention to the corner cabinets. "They'd be perfect in the two corners of the dining room where the windows don't interfere with the wall space they'd need... that is, if I could find a pecan dining set to complement them."

"Are you going to buy them?" Greg inquired, interested to see how Andrea did her shopping.

Andrea seemed startled by the inquiry. "What? Oh, of course not. I haven't got that kind of money. It'll be at least a year before I can afford anything like this."

Taken aback, Greg couldn't help asking, "Then what are we doing here? These will be long gone by then."

She responded pertly, "This is called window-shopping. Getting to know the market before you make any decisions. It's fun, and you never know, they may still be here. Some of these things have been here as long as I've been coming. And that's several years."

"But if the turnover is so low, how do they make any money?"

"I read an article in the paper written about them a while back. Don't lose any sleep over it. They do just fine." Her fingers trailed lovingly over the finely grained wood as she moved on. Halfway down the aisle she stopped again. Gesturing toward a dining-room table perched high on top of another, four small carpet squares under its four legs its only concession to preventing damage to the supporting tabletop, she questioned, "What do you think of that?"

Greg's mind was evidently already wandering, and he responded with a vague "What?" before looking around to see what Andrea was pointing at. Shaking his head negatively, he reminded her, "Only four chairs, and I don't see any leaves for extending the table."

Andrea chewed a fingertip thoughtfully. "Never thought of that. Still, if I bought that table, it might keep me from taking in any more strays for a while." Then she waved the thought away. "No, it would never work. Lack of space doesn't seem to deter me. We'd probably just end up eating in shifts or something." Determinedly she strode on.

"Uh, Andrea." Greg had to speak to her back as the aisles were too swollen with furniture and other odds and ends to allow walking abreast.

"Hmm?"

"Can we talk while we look through this junk?"

"It's not junk." Andrea was quick to correct him. "And we are talking. Or do you mean *talking*?"

"The latter."

"The old meaningful dialogue of college days gone by, hmm?" She fingered the intricacy of an ornately carved plaster-and-gilt picture frame before agreeing. "Okay, shoot."

"More specifically," he began in impersonal professional tones that already had Andrea cringing, "I would like to discuss some of what came up last night. You don't seem the narcissistic type who would overly worry about losing your figure or children messing up your place. The exact opposite, in fact." He seemed to grow less sure of himself as he went along. "I thought that if we could at least...talk about it...you know, so that I could try to understand what you were thinking along those lines..." The slightly uncertain wistfulness in his "Please?" took the sting from the formalness of the request, letting her see the vulnerability he sought to hide.

She turned and studied his face thoughtfully for a full thirty seconds, totally forgetting the Waterford Curraghmore pitcher she had spotted tucked away in an étagère off to one side. "Yeah, well, I guess this is as good a time as any. We may as well get it out of the way." She turned and walked a few steps while she gathered her thoughts, oblivious now to the furniture around her.

"Who's Peggy?"

Andrea whirled around. "How did you know she had anything to do with this?"

"It wasn't difficult." He shrugged. "When Karen lost her balance on the stairs, you called her Peggy and were upset way out of proportion to what actually happened. That, coupled with your evident fear of childbirth, leads me to believe something traumatic happened to a pregnant woman named Peggy, in all likelihood in front of you." He stopped, waiting for her to affirm or deny his assumption.

Absently she flicked an offending cobweb from her cheek and took care of the resulting itchy spot with a fingertip. "That's really very good," she commended. "You've managed to jump right into the crux of the matter."

"So tell me about it. Who is she?" he prodded.

Andrea answered slowly, thoughtfully. "She's my sister. There's Jenny, who's twenty-nine, and then Peggy, who turned thirty-two a month ago."

"And?" he prompted.

"Are you sure you want to hear this?"

"Yes." His tone was positive. "By the way, there's the table and chairs you want. See? It's in the same pecan tone as the corner cabinets we saw earlier."

She turned to challenge him. "I thought you wanted to hear about my deep-seated childhood neurosis."

"Oh, I do. I do. I also don't want to ruin your shopping expedition. Look. It has fantastic gargoyles carved on the legs and two leaves for expansion. It's perfect. I bet those are the table pads that go with it, too. Now, go on. I'm quite capable of entertaining two thoughts at one time, you know."

"Are you being flip?" she demanded.

"No, I am not being flip," he said, growing exasperated. "I am merely trying to get into the spirit of the day. I thought that was what you wanted." He was becoming indignant now.

Mulling it over for a moment, Andrea decided to give him the benefit of the doubt. "Well, okay. It's just that I've never told anybody about this before. Here I am trying to be open, and then it seemed as if you weren't really interested." She examined the cause of their rift. "You're right," she admitted. "It would be a perfect match."

Curtly he steered her forward by the elbow. "I know. Now let's get back to Peggy."

It was probably silly to take these things so seriously. She forced herself to relax and tell the tale. Possibly it was all a question of putting things into perspective. It had been years ago, after all. "As I said, Peggy's thirty-two. That makes her eight years older than I. When she was nineteen, she had to get married. It broke my mother's heart, but Peggy was convinced it was true love and was ecstatic over the baby. How do you like that highboy?" Greg was right. There was no reason why they couldn't enjoy the outing and talk at the same time.

He gave it his full attention before commenting, "No. Too big for the room size."

Andrea looked at him with renewed respect. Again he was right. It was too big. "Maybe you're in the wrong field. Interior design might be right up your alley."

His impatient gesture made his opinion clear.

"Anyway, I thought it was all terribly romantic. Eleven-year-olds do, you know."

Greg nodded in agreement. It was practically a fact that girls of such an age sopped up anything smacking of romance.

"He was awfully good-looking." She sighed. "Just proves how deceiving looks can be, I guess."

"Meaning?"

"Meaning that when she was four months pregnant, she lost the baby. They'd only been married a month and were living with my parents until they could find an apartment they could afford." Andrea's voice dropped to a whisper as the painful memories came back. "Well, suffice it to say, she lost the baby. Ted, the stinker, was delighted. Seems Peggy and the pregnancy had interfered with his plans for his higher education. Night school wasn't fast enough for him. Since he had only married her because of the baby, he saw no reason to stick around after it was lost. He walked out the door and never looked back. Peggy was devastated, and believe me, so was I."

"I can imagine," Greg muttered sympathetically. "Eleven. Even little problems are monumental at eleven, but something like that..." His voice trailed off as he became lost in thought.

Chapter Seven

Andrea rubbed an irritated brimming eyelid while perusing the room in a distracted manner. "Yes, well, unless you want to go through those shelves of *National Geographic* back copies, why don't we head on back to the other building?"

Greg's vision momentarily settled on the magazines in question before he dismissed them. "No, I don't think so. Frankly, those things give me an inferiority complex. I keep wondering what I'm doing slogging away here when there are so many other exciting things to be done. Some of the spreads they do on the various explorers and remote corners of the earth only serve as full-living-color reminders of the humdrumness of my life." Purposefully he twined his fingers with hers and led her from the building and into the crisp fall air.

Breathing deeply, Andrea noted, "You don't realize how musty the air is in there until you come back out." Together, they began weaving their way through a stand of rusting refrigerators blocking the path to the outbuilding.

"You can't seriously be upset about not being an explorer, can you? My goodness, it's a struggle for you to face up to a mushroom; I can just imagine you with fried grasshoppers or bird's-nest soup."

"It's not very nice of you to continually harp on a man's few failings. Haven't you ever heard you can get much further building on a person's positive aspects?"

"First, I'm not sure how far I want to get, and second, I wasn't harping on your failings, I was merely pointing out that you are what you are, which is quite a lot, and there's no point bemoaning what you'll never be. From all accounts you're an excellent physician and there are many, many people out there who would kill to have any area at all of real competence. Some of them would settle for being best at jacks, if that's all that was available to them. You just remember about the grass being greener and all of that. You're a doctor; enjoy being a good doctor. My Uncle Jim, Dad's brother, wasted most of his working life hating his career choices. And the funny thing is, his discontent followed him to each new career. He has yet to figure out that it's a mental outlook that will never change unless he changes it himself, internally. The job has little or nothing to do with it."

She stopped to remove her elastic band from her hair and gather some errant strays into the shining mass trailing down her back before redoing the ponytail. "Sorry," she muttered, "I didn't mean to lecture, but you touched a sore point."

"Don't apologize," he ordered with a peculiar glint in his eyes as he watched her. "You've given me some fascinating insights. I'll have to think about what you've said. Food for thought, as it were." Once again, he gave her a strange glance. "You're quite deep. Not your stereotypical physical-education instructor interested only in muscles, are you?"

Watching him kick a soda can out of their path before holding the door to the second building open for her, Andrea sighed. "I'd like to belt you one for that prejudicial remark. We are not all brainless jocks. There's a lot of theory and philosophy behind what we do. I could quote parts of Socrates' dialectics, places where he said 'What a disgrace it is for man to grow old without ever seeing the beauty and strength of which his body is capable,' but I won't. I could quote Plato's *Republic*, 'Anyone who can produce the best blend of the physical and the intellectual sides of education and apply them to the training of character is producing harmony,' but I won't do that either. It wouldn't be fair since I have admittedly spent the better part of the past week attributing all kinds of unsavory characteristics to the stereotypical doctor and lumping you in with the worst of them, I might add."

"So kind of you to let me off the hook like that," Greg muttered ironically. He surveyed the cramped, crowded building and started determinedly down an aisle, viewing furniture stacked haphazardly, as much as three pieces high.

"Now that you've told me off again, let's get back to your sister's story." While turning sideways to squeeze past a bumper pool set jutting out into the aisle, he investigated the frame of a plaid-cushioned toboggan sled that wasn't in bad condition. "That happened when you were eleven, and you saw it as an eleven-year-old. It's time you went back now and viewed it through the eyes of an adult since it's obviously still coloring the way you view all male-female relationships. By the way, how did she lose the baby?"

"I don't really know. That's not really the type of thing that would be discussed in front of an eleven-year-old, you know."

"Hmm, you're right about that." Andrea watched the muscles of his thighs strain against his faded jeans while he crouched to check the count on the number of balls in the pocket of the bumper pool table. The rippling pull of his shirt as it clung to his shoulders and arms was fascinating.

"It's not really that important, I was just interested," he explained, rising from his squatting position and stretching to relieve a cramp. Andrea's heart immediately threw in three extra beats, maybe four. But who was counting? He eyed her levelly, making her feel like the quintessential emotional female, incapable of a logical thought. "But that's all moot anyhow. Just for conversation's sake, let's discuss the husband for a minute."

Now they were in front of a massive ornately carved slab of wood. Positioned in its middle was an oval, slightly distorted antique mirror. It was elegant, but seemingly useless. The whole piece was also in dire need of refinishing. What did one do with a box approximately seven or eight feet tall, five feet wide and a foot-and-a-half deep? Andrea's brow furrowed thoughtfully as she studied it.

Noting her puzzlement, Greg helpfully noted, "It's a bed."

"What?" Andrea turned a blank look up at him. "What does Peggy's husband have to do with beds?"

"Not her husband—this, right here. It's a Murphy bed."

Quickly, Andrea's amazed countenance turned back to the object in question. "You're kidding. Really? How does it work?"

Peggy's husband was relegated to the back burner while Greg showed her the mechanics of the bed. "Seriously. This side here with the mirror adds to the room's decor during the day when the bed is up against the wall. Then at night, you pull it down and inside, waiting for the lights to go out, is a double mattress just right for two. Perfect for some cramped area where you need the sleeping space but can't afford to lose the room during the day."

More intrigued by the erotic idea of a bed impatiently waiting behind the scenes for the two of them to put out the lights than the space-saving factor, Andrea only admitted, "I do have to kneel on the bed to open some of my dresser drawers. It would be nice to get the bed up out of the way when it's not in use, but three hundred and ninety-five dollars? And that doesn't include the mattress."

Greg shrugged. "I'm telling you, these things won't be here when you come back. The pieces I can tell you're interested in are one-of-a-kind things. They'll be gone if you don't snap them up." He said nothing further, only followed Andrea when she glared and stubbornly walked away.

Not willing to spoil the day by getting into a discussion of their divergent views on managing money, she prompted leadingly, "About Peggy's husband..."

Greg's look told her more clearly than words that he knew precisely what she was doing. Knowingly he took the bait. "Yes, about him." He gave her a considering look. "Has it ever occurred to you that you're still looking at him through an eleven-year-old's eyes? I wonder what you'd think of him if you met him today and saw him through the eyes of an adult." His hand raised to ward off her impending interruption. "No, now just think about it. You said it was terribly romantic and he was wildly handsome. But you also indicated that your sister was barely nineteen. Stop and logically think of the boys available to a girl just out of high school. By definition, he had to be pretty immature." Once again, his hand staved off her instantaneous rebuttal. "Before you say anything, let's try to get a hold of your sister's yearbook and see some pictures of the guy. I'm sure you're viewing him through rose-tinted glasses and that's why you were so disappointed when he walked. If you'd bother to ask your sister, she'd probably tell you it was the best thing that ever happened to her. Who'd want to spend the rest of her life married to a man who didn't love her?" He raised a questioning eyebrow at her. "Unless your sister suffers from some arrested form of adolescent unrequited hero worship."

Andrea bristled at the accusation, considering it unwarranted as he had never even met her sister. "Don't be ridiculous!"

His smile melted her anger as his arm slipped around her. "I thought not. Now let's get out of here. We can explore more outside if you want, but I need some fresh air again."

They left the stuffy confines of the building and began poking through an unexplored area. "Look at this!" Greg bellowed, startling Andrea with the intensity of his yell. "I've always wanted to own the Brooklyn Bridge, and the Golden Gate Bridge is the next best thing," he said enthusiastically. "Damnation, they've got the Arc de Triomphe, Big Ben and the leaning tower of Pisa, too! How am I going to make up my mind?"

Convinced she had just witnessed the simultaneous collapse of every brain cell in his head, Andrea edged closer to see what had precipitated the aberration. "What in the world are you ranting about?" she questioned, even as she realized what it must be. There, in lilliputian splendor before her, was an entire selection of obstacles, all that remained of some now defunct miniature golf course. Europe's and America's major landmarks were there, complete with holes for golf balls and signs warning of water hazards, and the rules for play.

"Greg?" she inquired dubiously. "You're not seriously thinking about buying that, are you?" In horrified fascination she watched the smirk on his handsome face grow. So much for her no-sense-of-humor accusation.

Greg was so engrossed in his study of the find that he didn't even hear her query. Instead, the cool November sun sent flashes of fire through his thick mahogany hair and he rocked on his heels, hands stuffed into his jeans pockets while he grinned a silly little grin. "How many times in a man's life," he asked rhetorically, "does an opportunity like this arise? The Golden Gate Bridge!"

"Snap out of it, Greg. You look like you're going into a trance!" Andrea burst out, trying to get through the smug bubble he had spun around himself upon spotting this treasure. "You can't possibly buy it."

That got through as nothing else could have. He frowned, and turned his attention to her. "Why not?" he demanded.

She took a deep breath. Why not? "Well, for one thing, it's totally impractical. What would you do with it? Use it for a car-hood ornament? It's six feet long! You have no place to put it," she pointed out triumphantly.

"Don't be such a stick-in-the-mud," he shot back before returning his attention to San Francisco's famous landmark. "We'll set up a miniature golf hole in the backyard. The kid next door, what's his name, Jimmy? would love it." That self-satisfied smirk was growing again. He rubbed his hands together in delight before abruptly turning about and starting off toward the main building, leaving Andrea to stumble and stutter after him. "Come on. I'm going to buy it. Nobody in their right mind would pass by the chance to own San Francisco's Golden Gate Bridge."

"But you can't. What if you get an apartment with no yard available? What will you do with it then? After all, you're only staying until Karen has had the baby, remember?" Andrea's voice was acquiring a certain desperate quality. She simply couldn't believe anybody would throw away a hundred dollars on a miniature golf hazard.

Greg didn't even break stride. "Has anyone ever told you that you have a basically negative personality? All your can'ts and shouldn'ts are causing you to miss out on an awful lot of the spontaneous fun of living."

"What? Look who's talking!" Andrea blurted out. It was unbelievable that the original straight man was accusing *her* of being no fun. Of all the nerve.

"Okay, so I have some catching up to do. But who's doing the complaining now that I'm making a stab at it, hmm? You can't have it both ways, my dear. Now close your mouth," he directed after a look over his shoulder informed him that her generous lower lip was hanging down in stupefaction. "And let's search out whoever we have to pay so we can locate a hamburger place. Lunch should have been two hours ago. I'm starved."

"I never finished telling you about Peggy's Ted," Andrea called after his retreating back.

"So tell me in the car," he told her in a disinterested tone. Clearly his main interest now lay in claiming his bridge, as if someone else would snatch up the dumb thing before he could get to it, she thought furiously.

"It's now or never," she threatened, thoroughly irritated with him.

He turned to her with a facade of patient forbearance. "Okay, what about him? The guy was a jerk. There's little that can be added to that."

"You know how you said because he married a nineteen-year-old he had to be, by definition, immature?"

"Yeah?"

"That I was only looking at him through an eleven-year-old's rose-tinted glasses?"

"Yeah?"

"He was a junior at the University of Chicago. In premed."

Greg looked back at her with a glint of humor in the depths of his eyes. "I really must look the man up someday," he promised. "Not only has he made you afraid of childbirth and its tandem effect on marriage, but he's also managed to make you afraid of marriage in general and doctors in particular. I have a lot to take up with the man, should we ever meet. Right now, however, I have a bridge to buy, so if you'll excuse me..."

He laughed outright as Andrea refused to accompany him, stomping off instead toward the car. "Damn, pompous *M.D.*," she muttered under her breath as she strode off, the appellation M.D. coming off as a particularly vile invective.

Greg found her there quite a bit later, the entire contents of her purse now dumped over the car's bright yellow hood. He sighed as he took in her bent form foraging through the morass of coupons, pens and loose change that had escaped from her wallet, listened to her mumbled soliloquy on the ancestry and disgusting personal habits of car keys. Clearly, she was in need of a caretaker—someone who would at the least keep track of her shoes and have a spare set of car keys available at all times. "They're in your pocket," he informed her in a kind tone, which she took immediate exception to.

"They're not," she snarled back. "I already checked." And she turned her jacket pocket inside out to show him. "And stop looking so darn smart. If we don't find them, we could be stranded here forever."

"It only took us a little over an hour to get here. Surely it would only take Tim an equal amount of time to rescue us," he pointed out with calm logic. "Now check your pants pocket, which is what I had in mind in the first place."

"They're not there. I never put my— Don't say a word," she instructed as her slender fingers withdrew the offending key from her jeans back pocket.

"Had you sat down, I'm sure you would have found them without any help," he offered solicitously, but she only sniffed haughtily in response.

It was fortunate that Friday was a busy day for Andrea. She tried to stay away from mirrors, afraid of seeing steam rising from her ears. It was hard to ignore her reflection in the aerobics class, though. "To the left, two, three, four. And right...." She ignored the wall of mirrors and tried to dance the edge off her frustrations, exhorting her class to follow.

Had she actually considered anything deeper than a surface relationship with that lunatic? He had kept up an innocent facade while repeating the trading-post owner's directions to a truck rental place. He had totally ignored her protestations that the bridge was only about six feet long. It was a small-scale replica of the real thing, not the real thing itself. Surely they could manage to get it into the car somehow. And the trailer he had rented was definitely a gross case of overkill...

"Now twist. Keep those backs straight."

Her fury had taken root and grown as she watched the men struggle with first the two massive corner cabinets she had admired, the dining-room set Greg had discovered, the old-fashioned Murphy bed that would take weeks to refinish, the bumper pool table, the toboggan and then finally, San Francisco's Golden Gate Bridge.

"What do you think you're doing?" she had hissed in his ear while he was tucking in the table pads and using them to keep the pieces from knocking together during the long ride home.

He had shrugged. "Well, I'll need furniture when I get an apartment. You can store it for me until I need it...."

"Two circles now. Fast runners in the front of the gym, slow runners in the back...."

"Greg," she had implored on a note of panic. "Think about this. How are you going to pay for all this? You've just spent at least two thousand dollars. You've already got loans from your schooling."

Greg had spoken firmly. "Don't insult me by casting me in your father's role. I know exactly how much I've charged to my credit-card bill and what my monthly loan payments are. I'm not getting in over my head."

"But—" Andrea had begun desperately.

"There are no buts about it," he had affirmed implacably. "And you may as well know right now that those kitchen cabinets you were foolishly going to let go are arriving tomorrow. Tim and I will install them over the weekend. He's taking out the old ones while we're out today."

"What?" she'd gasped.

"You heard me. I went over Monday while you were at work. You were right. They'd adapt perfectly to your kitchen dimensions. It's ridiculous to pass up a bargain like that. For heaven's sake, they're practically giving that display away."

"I suppose you're lending me those too?" she had questioned sarcastically. "Going to take them with you to your new apartment as well...?"

"Back to your places now for thirty jumping jacks," she directed her class. Slowly, some of the worst of her anger was working its way out as she returned to her memory....

"I'll rent them to you for the next few months with option to buy. How's that?" he'd said.

He had looked disgusted with the entire direction of the conversation. Well, too bad for him.

The women in the early-morning class were looking at her strangely, and she realized she had lost count and must be past the usual thirty jumping jacks limit. "Sorry," she muttered, changing into a two-count forward kick. "Now back, one, two, and side, one, two. Opposite side. Again, forward..."

By the time four o'clock rolled around, Andrea felt that she would at least be able to speak to the occupants of her home in a civil manner. Her feelings of anger were unwarranted and short-lived.

"Hi." Greg kissed her on the forehead as she tossed her purse and books on the old Formica table, all that remained of the kitchen she had worked in only the day before.

"Hi, yourself," she grunted ungraciously, all her former ire returning at the sight of her gutted kitchen.

Greg was intent on ignoring her surly behavior and indicated the books on the table with a stab of his thumb. "I didn't think PE instructors did homework. What are the books for?"

Andrea chose not to rise to the slur, instead answering his question straight out. "Two of my seventh graders have been diagnosed with early curvature of the spine," she related. "I want to make sure none of the things we do in class would be detrimental. I also want to find out if there's anything I could add—stretching exercises or something that would help them out."

He was obviously impressed. "Where were the teachers like you when I was in school?" he inquired.

Andrea was not in the mood to be impressed by his compliments, however, and made a disparaging noise in the back of her throat. Looking around in the sure knowledge that she had utterly lost any control of her life, she asked, "How are things going?"

"Not bad, not bad. Tim's home from class. He'll be down as soon as he's changed his clothes. We'll work for the next hour and a half or so bringing in the new cabinets. I've got them all uncrated and the floor marked off as to where they go. I thought we'd go to a burger place for dinner and then to the Pinewood Derby. Jimmy says it starts at seven. I know our car is going to win," he predicted in happy anticipation. "My car always got a ribbon when I was a Scout. After that, I noticed in the Park District brochure that there's a free lecture on birding tonight at eight o'clock and a walk tomorrow morning at the Keay Nature Center."

Andrea looked blankly at Karen who had just entered the room with the level Greg had sent her to find. "Birding? Is that like hunting? I hate hunting of any type. I'm not going to trap innocent little birds. You know who'd get stuck cleaning the feathers off. You can forget it. The whole idea makes me gag."

Laughingly Karen explained, "Birding only requires a pair of binoculars. It has nothing to do with killing the little dears, merely identifying them. Greg's to the point where he can stay awake all day now." Greg grimaced at the way his niece made him sound like a five-year-old finally able to give up his afternoon nap. "Today he actually couldn't fall asleep when he lay down and ended up reading me bits and pieces of a birding manual. Fascinating stuff."

Karen yawned meaningfully. "It seems there are over six hundred species of birds indigenous to the continental United States. Birders keep track of how many they can spot."

"Sounds real boring." Andrea looked at Greg in wide-eyed wonder. Was he actually going to insist they do this?

"He's trying to show you what a fun person he is, I think," Karen answered her while rolling her eyes expressively.

Knowing full well what his response would be, Andrea shut her eyes in resignation and plaintively questioned, "It's such a cold, ugly night, couldn't we stay home and read the encyclopedia instead? It would have to be more entertaining than a birding lecture, for heaven's sake."

"And who spent yesterday lecturing me about my attitude? Hmm?" Greg held the level to the cabinet he had wrestled into place and leaned to make an adjustment in its position. "Buck up, it won't be so bad."

"Geez, Louise. I know I owe you one. But birding? I ask you...."

"Tsk, tsk, my dear. Watch that mental attitude of yours."

In the end, Andrea capitulated. After all, he had been a good sport the day before, even if she had been madder than hell at him over the high-handed tactics he had employed and his inability to grasp anything but the loosest idea of financial stability. She did insist on fried chicken instead of burgers, though, as the thought of the latter reminded her of yesterday's lunch, which in turn reminded her of yesterday in general, and that memory made her blood boil. *The Golden Gate Bridge, indeed!*

Jimmy proudly introduced his parents to Greg while ushering them all into the grammar school's gymnasium. In barely controlled excitement he pointed out the extended length of assembled track sitting in splendor in the middle of the gym's wooden floor. The air hummed in hushed anticipation, the level rising each time a blue-shirted Scout entered the room and stood in line to register his car. The tension was almost palpable by the time Jimmy's den was called for their race. Greg squeezed his hand, instructing him not to worry as the cars were set behind the gate at the high end of the track. Several Scouts averted their faces, unable to watch as three fathers drafted to act as judges leaned over the finish line, waiting to pick out the first three cars while the official starter dropped the gate, allowing the cars to start down the track.

The pressure Greg's hand exerted on Andrea's waist increased noticeably as he and Jimmy intently watched their car finish first by one-sixteenth of a length. A first place in either the second or third heat would put them up for the races deciding best of pack and entry into the divisional championship derby against other troops in the area.

"The whole trick," Greg confided to Andrea as Jimmy's car clinched best of den, "is the wheels. You have to be sure to sand any burrs off the nails holding the wheels to the car and nail them in perfectly straight, but not too tightly. Then be sure to keep the paint when you decorate the car away from the wheels, and no glue near them, either. Finally, a little powdered graphite to help them spin freely." Andrea filed the information away in her useless-trivia fund while Greg took his graphite tube from his shirt pocket and blew a little more into the car's critical areas.

Greg was as proud as any parent when it finally came time to determine best of pack. Andrea knew he would make a good father. His ego was obviously strong enough to allow him to come down to a kid's own level without feeling silly about it, as evidenced by the real enjoyment he was having this evening. The car ran beautifully the first time down, finishing first easily. Jimmy clenched his father's hand on one side and squeezed Greg's on the other as the gate lifted for the second run. Andrea watched in disbelief as their six-inch streak of silver spit off a wheel halfway down the track, skidding to a distant sixth finish. Frantically, Jimmy and his father worked to tap the recalcitrant nail and wheel back in for the third heat, Greg diplomatically remaining in the background. Andrea could see his fingers spasmodically moving, echoing each adjustment made by John McKnight.

Greg's exhorted "Come on, you stinker!" was barely discernible as the cars were set up for the third heat. It was a disaster. As if the manufacturer's warranty had just expired, three of the midget cars simultaneously lost wheels immediately. They careened down the runway in a race all their own, jumping their grooves and jamming adjacent cars. Jimmy's pride and joy had developed a vindictive show-them spirit of its own, spewing one wheel after another, finally sliding on its bottom to a third-place finish in spite of itself.

"See?" Greg grinned. "My cars always show."

All concern over the lost wheels were forgotten as Jimmy threw himself into his mother's arms, screaming, "We made the finals! We did it!"

When he was finally calm, his manners were remembered and Greg and Andrea were soberly thanked for all their efforts with a mature handshake. Andrea looked wryly at her hand. A handshake instead of a kiss? Jim confided, "The cookies were the best part, Miss Conrades," before stipulating, "especially since Mrs. Nyland wasn't hurt." She guessed he didn't want to appear totally callous, even at his young age. Watching him shake hands with Greg in as adult a fashion as he could muster, Andrea couldn't help but realize that if Jimmy had been Greg's own son, he wouldn't have had to remember his manners. The boisterous finale would have automatically included him. He would have done the last-minute repairs and shared in the victory celebration from its inception and not just as a tacked-on "you too" remembrance. Come to think of it, had it been her son as well as Greg's, the heartfelt hug and excited kisses would have gone to her, too—and for no other reason than that she was his mother. Who else would a child turn to in the thrill of victory? Sharing totally in *your own* child's every emotional peak and valley...it was an exceedingly heavy thought.

Chapter Eight

Andrea hadn't said much during the short car ride to the Park District's building where the birding lecture was to be given. Pondering the wonder of her own progeny hadn't left her much in the mood for conversation. Not only was she worried about childbirth per se, but how would she ever figure out if Greg was in love with love or with her? What a mess.

In the lecture hall itself, her thoughts slowly churned. Whole new concepts were taking root and growing in inverse proportion to the strength of the gradually dimming lights.

"Welcome to tonight's introduction to birding. Our talk tonight will be followed by a birding walk tomorrow morning. For those of you able to participate, we will meet in the Keay Nature Center parking lot at eight in the morning."

What would it be like to have her own child? To share a child, she revised, as the feat was impossible on her own. Any sophomore biology student could tell her that. She'd need help to accomplish anything along those lines. Her child. And Greg's. A child conceived with Greg. She turned to study him with a new perspective.

"Aristotle was one of the first birdwatchers of record, cataloging approximately one hundred and seventy species. Of course, he was not the first to watch birds. They play prominently in early man's cave drawings in Spain and France, Egyptian hieroglyphics and ancient Chinese potteries. Science then was liberally mixed with fancy. Birds' flight and feeding patterns were carefully watched for the omens the Greeks and Romans sought. Our word auspicious comes to us from the Latin *avis*—bird—and *specere*—to look at."

Andrea had made it a habit to refrain from coyness. Her instinctive honesty acknowledged that she was attractive. Up to now, it had been very much her own choice to remain uninvolved. But Greg wasn't allowing her to brush him off as easily as she had the others. More and more, she was questioning whether she really wanted to. He had his faults, true, but didn't she? In the anonymity of the darkened room, she detachedly measured the man beside her. Starting with the thick thatch of deep brown curls he despaired of ever taming, and continuing down the silhouette of his brow and lineal patrician nose, her vision descended feature by feature, finding nothing to criticize until she at last reached the white athletic shoes with their three green stripes. Ah, no one could ignore the size of the feet sprawled out in front of that chair. Size thirteen, at least. Her triumph was short-lived, however, as she sorrowfully admitted to herself how truly picayune that one flaw was.

Clinically there was every possibility that she and Greg could produce a brood of rather spectacular children. That was the honest truth. But getting there from where she was now was something else entirely.

"Why study birds? We could get into the explorer's cliché, 'because they are there.' It's valid enough, but there can be so much more to it..."

Could she bring herself to go to bed with the man? She knew the facts of life; she taught adolescent girls. It was her job to know. Many of them felt far more at ease talking to the female physical-education instructor than to their parents or the male science teacher. She took another covert look at Greg. He seemed oblivious to her internal turmoil, having eyes only for the speaker.

"Birds can be an early index of trouble in the food pyramid. Many environmental effects of chemicals first appeared in the bird populations...."

The problem was that children weren't had clinically. Greg would never allow any test-tube babies while he was warm and breathing. And well on the road to recovery now, there was no question of his being anything but warm and breathing. His body radiated its warmth in heated waves, pulling and tugging at her, beckoning her toward his glowing center. Could he possibly be as oblivious to the magnetic pull he emanated as he seemed? His total concentration seemed to be on Darwin's theory of evolution having roots in studies of a certain Pacific island's ground-finch population.

What would it be like to sleep with Greg? Not merely the slumber implied in the rigid definition of their act on his second night in her home, but sleeping with him in the fullest sense of the word, with all the opulent and fertile connotations it gained when applied to a man and woman together.... To sleep with Greg. Previously, when thinking in terms of sleeping with a man, she had always thought of it in more or less a generic sense—with man, in the abstract.

Now suddenly, with the thought of a flesh-and-blood man beside her—with Greg beside her, she decided that it might be sort of fun. In fact it might be downright pleasurable, erotically speaking. Erotic... now there was a word by definition rich in its sensual implications.

"In the words of Henry Beston, 'We need another wiser and perhaps more mystical concept of animals. We patronize them for their incompleteness, for their tragic fate of having taken form so far below ourselves. And therein we err, and greatly err. For the animal should not be measured by man. In a world older and more complete than ours they move finished and complete, gifted with extensions of the senses we have lost or never attained, living by voices we shall never hear. They are not brethren, they are not underlings. They are other nations caught with ourselves in the net of life and time, fellow prisoners of the splendor and travail of the earth.' "

My gosh. She was all set to tiptoe naked through the tulips and the speaker was waxing philosophical. Anyone who found a lecture on birds sensually stimulating was in dire need of mental aid. A psychiatrist. One with a great deal of experience in lost causes would be best.

"Uh, Greg?" Andrea whispered in his ear, "I'll be right back, okay?" He nodded absently and Andrea was off her chair, heading for the door, her shadow temporarily blotting out the projector's thrown image of a red-winged blackbird. It was some sort of native to the area.

She went to the ladies' room and washed her face with cold water. The irony of the situation was almost too much. She, who was always so cold during the winter months, was overheated now in late November. That alone was enough to convince her that she needed help....

Back in her seat she found that concentrating on each slide made the rest of the bird lecture manageable, if not exactly inspiring. Still, Andrea breathed a sigh of relief when it was all over. Greg's arm rested naturally across her shoulders as he lightly guided her to the car.

"Did you enjoy yourself?" he enquired politely as he leaned forward to start the engine.

"Oh, yes. I particularly liked the Shakespearean freak wreaking havoc on our native birds by importing and releasing the starlings into New York's Central Park because Will mentioned them in his plays."

"That was interesting, wasn't it?" he asked, obviously delighted in his assumption that she had found the talk intriguing.

"Oh, yes," she repeated. "Listen, do you think we could stop for some ice cream and root beer to bring home? I'm awfully hot."

Greg looked at her in surprise. It was anything but warm outside. While the car heater was good, it wasn't *that* efficient. But he didn't question her, rather he turned into a midnight market's parking lot. "Do we need anything else? Bread? Milk?"

"Mmm, no, I don't think so. Well, maybe you'd better get some painkillers, too."

Concerned with her request coupled with the seeming hot flashes, Greg placed a professional hand on her forehead. "You don't feel warm. Are you sick?"

"Uh, no. It's just that, um, we're out of them, and...they're good to have around...just in case...you know." She didn't know if she was sick or not. Anything was possible at this point. She certainly felt weird, and it would certainly be easier to blame her problems on a bug rather than the effect Greg had on her. Darn it, she wasn't even married yet, and she still had no privacy. She needed time alone, just to think. Maybe she could send them all out tomorrow. The Cubs and Sox had made a run for the baseball pennant, but the season had run out before they'd made good their threat. That left the Bears, but football was played on Sunday and Monday nights. She'd have to think of something else.

While waiting for Greg to emerge from behind the *Chicken Whole Fryers Only 49¢/lb* sign that was plastered across one of the brightly lit storefront windows, Andrea put her head back against the seat's headrest and meditated on her life's recent turns. Now that Tim and Karen had moved upstairs, she mused, it was going to be increasingly difficult to maintain any type of distance, emotional or otherwise, as far as Greg was concerned. The sixty-four-thousand-dollar question was, Did she really want to? Lately, her body seemed to have a mind of its own, openly rebelling against the restrictions it had lived under for so long. She had been slow in her development all her life. Maybe this was some type of delayed adolescence hitting her.

She doubted it. She suspected it had more to do with Greg himself and the kind of man he was, rather than the status of some unbalanced hormone coursing through her bloodstream. Watching Greg appear, it seemed only right that the automated doors should swing open without his touching them. After all, her heart raced and her pulse slammed inside her veins without his touching her. Perhaps he was some heretofore unknown god recently descended from Olympus. Perhaps they could bottle him and sell his essence...Eau de Greg toilet water. It would beat musk hands down. She smiled at her own whimsy. Greg gave a bemused grin of his own in response as he slid through the open car door.

"Did you miss me?" he questioned, leaning over for a quick kiss.

Andrea found herself answering honestly, "As a matter of fact, I did. In the span of one short week, you have managed to thoroughly worm your way into my life. The car did seem empty without you." She sounded a little surprised.

Greg seemed pleased and gave her another kiss—one that wasn't so quick.

The house was dark upon their return. Apparently, Karen and Tim had decided to make an early night of it. Andrea and Greg quietly drank their black cows, sipping up the root beer as it foamed in response to the ice cream. She noticed the way Greg kept trying to set up meaningful eye contact, but her own slid uneasily away. She just wasn't quite ready. Finally, she withdrew and closed herself in the bathroom to get ready for bed.

The navy and beige shower curtain had just swished over the rod behind her, enclosing her in the privacy of the tub, when she heard the bathroom door gently crack open. She was going to have to install a lock on the damn door if she was going to make it through the next few months.

"Can I come in?" Greg's head poked around the door.

"Would it matter if I said no?" She sighed in resignation.

Cheerfully, his response came as he entered the room. "Not really. I need a shower too. I thought we'd conserve water. The government's environmental agency would approve."

"That's probably why our taxes are so high—too much regulation."

"Come on," he urged. "It'll be fun."

"Can't you wait ten minutes?"

"Brother, what a party pooper. Oh, all right. I'll wait outside the door. But I'm going to leave the door open a few inches so we can talk. Okay? I think it's time." She felt the draft of the door once again being opened and took a quick peek around the edge of the shower curtain. She could just catch a glimpse of a jeans-clad leg. He must have settled on the hall floor just outside the door.

"Now it's occurred to me from some remarks that Karen and Tim have made and my own observations that you're not used to a lot of hugging and touching. You keep shying away from me. Here's how I see it. I shower; I use deodorant. You shower; you use deodorant. I'm attractive. You're attractive."

Andrea wondered if he'd ever been on the debating team in that high school in Pennsylvania. He would have been a killer. He could carry on both sides of the debate all by himself.

"I like you, you like me. There's no real reason for you to back away all the time. That mess your sister was involved in just doesn't cut it as reason enough. You want to know what I think?"

She could hardly wait. "What?" she answered obligingly and began to rinse her hair. She had used too much shampoo and her head refused to stop foaming.

She was right to have been leery because Greg continued, "It's just that most women, men too for that matter, even if they remain virgins, have at least experienced a little petting as teenagers. That way, the path is paved for further intimacy when they're ready. But I suspect you're starting from scratch. What you need, and what I intend to provide, is a little remedial fondling to sort of get you used to my touch gradually. Before you know it," he cheerfully informed her, "I'll have you totally addicted. You won't be able to live without it. So what do you think of my analysis?"

Andrea sputtered under her cascading bubbles. The man was too much. "I've had some boyfriends, you conceited clod," she replied defensively. She hadn't allowed them much freedom with their hands, but she'd had a few. Reaching from behind the curtain, she snagged a towel and wrapped herself better than a mummy before stepping from behind the curtain.

"I love you, you know," Greg said after seeing her and laughing. "Here I thought that when I finally got around to deciding to settle down, it would take me several years of research to find the kind of woman I needed. I'm very picky, you know. Not too easy to get along with, either."

There was no need to state the obvious. She felt bad enough about falling for him without his rubbing her face in it.

"And instead," he continued conversationally, "here you fall out of the sky and into my lap. The perfect woman. Manna from heaven, as it were." She could see him unbuttoning his shirt out in the hallway through the partially opened door.

"That's ridiculous," Andrea contradicted him. "The whole thing is very earthbound. I did not fall from the sky. You tumbled in *my* front door. And without being terribly pleasant about it, I might add." She might as well get the story straight, she thought.

Greg ignored her. "As I was saying, who would have thought? Just as I'm ready to actively campaign for a wife, the perfect candidate shows up. Terrific sense of humor; good, if unorthodox cook..."

He would have to qualify any compliment, she thought.

"Good-looking, sexy as hell, loves children. Perfect," he concluded, as he reentered the bathroom and stepped around Andrea to toss his shirt on the radiator.

Andrea watched as he began removing his undershirt and her mouth went dry at the magnificent torso being bared in front of her. She quickly left the room. Greg should stop and listen to himself talk, she thought as she rubbed herself dry in her bedroom. She had been too angry over his buying the Golden Gate Bridge the other day to finish the talk she had planned. And it still sounded to her as though once the burden of medical training was over and he was ready to make a family commitment, he were grabbing the first person of the female variety to pass by, rationalizing as he did so that she was the woman of his dreams. She was starting to suspect buckteeth, four eyes and cooties would have been passed off as inconsequential. He was ready to settle down, in capital letters.

Toweling her hair, she thought about the man left behind in the shower and was stabbed with a fierce longing, somewhat akin, she suspected, to Eve's consideration of a certain apple in a certain garden. There wasn't another woman within a ten-mile radius of that soap-slicked tub, Andrea postulated, that wouldn't grab with both hands the opportunity standing literally at her fingertips and head for the nearest clergyman. She sighed. She wasn't most women. It was doubtful she could give him the things he craved—home and hearth...children...the unfailing love and devotion every marital participant deserved.

Greg reappeared in an amazingly short period of time wrapped in one of her new burgundy-red towels. Speaking from her doorway, he continued the conversation as though there had been no interruption, assuring her, "Not to worry. I won't rush you while you're feeling harassed. I know what I want, and I intend to get it, but I'll give you the time you need, too."

"How much time?" she questioned suspiciously. He was being entirely too accommodating, considering what she'd already seen of his personality.

"Ohh, at least another day or two." Her lips were pinched as she watched him turn away to hum jauntily on his way down the hall to his own room.

Andrea took advantage of his absence to blow her hair dry in the steamy bathroom, aiming the dryer first at the mirror to clear it of its moisture-laden fog, and next at her own thick locks. Then she went back to her bedroom and flicked her electric blanket to five as she passed the bed en route to the dresser. It was chilly in the house and going to get worse. The new thermostat automatically set the heat back to fifty-five in the evening. With that in mind, she knelt on the end of the bed, giving herself enough room to open the dresser drawer and remove a floor-length red and black plaid flannel nightgown, its collar and cuffs trimmed with delicate white lace.

Just as she was about to unwind the large towel and unfold the gown to change, Greg waltzed into the room, sporting nothing but a ratty pair of old pajama bottoms that clung to his hipbones and seemed to stay there by force of habit.

Clutching the towel tightly to her slight bosom, she gasped in affronted dignity, almost as though they hadn't just shared the bathroom. "What are you doing in here?"

Greg frowned in an offended, displeased manner at the blanket control box where a glowing red light mutely testified to its bed-heating capabilities. "Nasty things, electric blankets," he commented as he followed the cord to its outlet. He reached down and gave a self-satisfying yank, effectively cutting off its power source. Rechecking the control box, he seemed pleased by its blank face. "I'm quite sure anyone interested in doing a bit of research would discover a direct relationship between the rise in the divorce rate and the advent of artificial bed-warming devices."

"To a certain portion of the population, artificial means are all that's available," Andrea responded in a saccharine tone.

"Here's where I intend to demonstrate another of the benefits of having a husband. Get into the bed," he directed, pulling down the blankets and spread with one hand while pointing to her flannel nightie with the other. "And get rid of that. I'll chuck these," he indicated his worn bottoms with a flick of his hand, "And we'll keep each other warm."

Andrea ignored him, snapped the nightgown free of its neat folds and prepared to slip it over her head. "Greg, every night at ten-thirty the temperature drops to fifty-five degrees in here. I'm freezing. Now kindly get out of my room so I can go to bed. I'm not in the mood for any more games."

"Andrea, Andrea," Greg admonished sorrowfully. "When will you ever learn? I am not playing games with you. You told me yourself I didn't know how." He plucked the gown from her grasp and pushed her toward the bed. "Now get rid of the towel and get into bed."

He held up a placating hand as he saw the promise of rebellion flash in her blue eyes. "I just want to hold you and cuddle a little during the night. Come on, humor me, I'm a sick man."

If only he *were* still sick. Now, well on the road to recovery, he was becoming more and more difficult to handle. If she thought events were slipping out of her control a week ago, they were child's play in comparison to this. Here was a scene she couldn't have dreamed in her wildest imaginings. "I don't care how much body heat you radiate. During the winter I sleep in a flannel gown, knee socks, the electric blanket on medium and sometimes even a robe. You're going to tell me you can replace all that?"

Greg sat on the edge of the bed contemplating her blue-tinged lips. "Knee socks, too, hmm? I had no idea things were that bad. Let's feel your feet." Obligingly, Andrea placed her right foot high on his thigh while she waited expectantly for him to pass judgment. She bit her lower lip to keep from laughing out loud as he paled in the face of the icy-cold invasion of a rather intimate area. Quickly he grabbed it away and held her foot between two warm hands. "Yes, well—" he cleared his throat and started again generously offering "—tell you what. You go ahead and put some socks on. But no nightie. Think of it as a scientific evaluation of the principles of the Indians of Tierra del Fuego. Didn't they all sleep with their feet toward the fire with the idea that if their feet were warm, their bodies soon would be as well?"

Trust Greg to put her first night nude in his arms into *National Geographic* terms. Andrea sighed and reached into the drawer for a pair of thick, bright red knee-highs, the action signifying her capitulation. It just wasn't worth the trouble to keep fighting. She, who had managed to keep men at a distance all these years, was about to share a bed with a man who made her crazy. She inserted both thumbs into the top of the sock, rolling it up between thumbs and fingers, and bent over to insert her toe. The tuck in the top of her towel responsible for holding the togalike arrangement together began to loosen, and she didn't bother to make a stab at refastening it. It wasn't worth the effort. He was going to win by simply wearing her down.

His dark eyes flared with copper sparks in anticipation of the towel's ultimate capitulation. "This could get good. We may have just come across the up-and-coming replacement for black stockings and garter belts."

"Shut up," she advised, thinking to herself, like heck he was going to win. She called upon that one percent of her backbone that didn't consist of mush, grabbed the flannel granny gown and slipped it over her head. She removed the towel from under the safety of its bulky folds and slid between the sheets, shivering as the cool percale made contact with her few uncovered areas. "Couldn't we have the blanket on for just a few minutes? Sort of preheat the sheets?" she queried plaintively.

Not even bothering to remove his pajamas, Greg climbed in beside her with a frown and nestled up to her back, spoon fashion, pulling her against him to improve the fit. "No. We'll be warm in no time. Think of all the energy we're saving."

The truth of the matter was, he did seem to be emitting an awful lot of heat. She was starting to feel incredibly warm, and that warmth seemed to focus around the hand that draped around her to cup a small but firm breast in its gently callused palm. She snuggled back farther against him. This was better than old-fashioned Victorian warming bricks by a long shot. "What are you doing?" she murmured sleepily.

His head lifted from its desultory shoulder-nibbling activities. "I'm kissing what should be your lovely alabaster shoulders. It's supposed to be sexy. It's just hard to properly pull off through all this fabric."

She stifled a giggle at his hurt tone and hastened to assure him, "Oh, it's very erotic, truly it is." She squirmed a little farther backward. He really was as good as an electric blanket any night of the week. Greg gasped as she snuggled more deeply. His hands began to roam a bit and he moaned under his breath. Andrea was sure it was just this type of situation her mother had warned her against when she'd shown her first interest in boys years before. "Uh, Greg?" she gasped. "Maybe this wasn't such a great idea." Anything that felt this good must be wrong, and she was sure her mother would agree with that sentiment.

Greg pulled her around, denying her claim. The imprisoning ropes of his arms held her to his lanky length, aggressively burning her with the undeniable proof of his arousal. "Oh, no, sweetheart. We've just immeasurably improved on the original concept." A shudder ran through him as his mouth closed over her own trembling lips. One hand eased under her nightie before holding her more tightly against the cradle of his hips, impressing the strength of his desire upon her in no uncertain terms.

"Oh, Andrea," he muttered against the softness of her mouth. "I thought I could hold you, lead you gradually into wanting what I want, but I can't." He leaned back to try to read her face in the dark. One hand cradled her head by her ear, its thumb stroking from the bridge of her nose along the line of her high cheekbone. He kept their hips in tight contact while he implored her, "Make up your mind now. Tell me if you don't want me to touch you. Now, while there's still a remote possibility of stopping."

It was Andrea's turn to search the darkened planes of his face for answers. She couldn't read his face in the room's velvet darkness. What did he want from her? "Greg?" she asked uncertainly. She could feel his body tense, awaiting her rejection.

"I want to be the one to show you, Andrea. Let me be the only one to know your sweetness... Please. Let it be now."

Suddenly, none of it mattered anymore. She would probably spend the rest of her life coaxing his smiles and avoiding bankruptcy court, but to spend even one night wrapped in his arms like this would somehow be worth it. What she felt for the dark man holding her so closely transcended mere liking, leaving it behind as inconsequential.

"Yes, Greg," she breathed, hardly able to take in the import of what she was saying. "I want you to be the one. Show me. Show me now."

"Thank you," Greg offered humbly, slipping her flannel covering up and off, and immediately lowering his generous full lips to the creamy skin of her neck. "You won't regret this. I promise I'll take care of you. Always."

Andrea didn't argue the ridiculousness of his vow because his marauding mouth was wreaking havoc on her sanity as it worked its way down her body fastening itself finally upon the peak of one quivering, swollen breast. "Do you like this, Andrea?" His sensitive fingers joined in, adeptly tormenting the other nipple, and Andrea gasped at the strength of the sensations he was able to produce. No one had ever touched her so intimately. No one but Greg had successfully breached the barricades.

Slowly her own hands began moving, seeming to have an innate knowledge of what to do to bring him pleasure. They skimmed the surface of his broad back, barely touching the warm skin, making him shiver in response. Taking heart, she moved on, allowing her sensitive fingertips to smoothly glide down the distance of his muscled arms and then onto the firmly delineated planes of his chest, provoking each newfound territory with teasing little circles.

Momentarily stopping his feasting, Greg paused, giving all his attentions to cataloguing the intense feelings her touch caused to surface. Andrea welcomed the respite as her senses threatened to overload. She closed her eyes, waiting for him to continue. A moment later, she regretfully opened them, a sense of foreboding telling her that she was not to know the fruits of her momentous decision. "Greg?" she questioned uncertainly.

Greg looked torn in half, pain furrowing his brow as he collapsed on his back next to her. "It's not enough," he said.

"What are you talking about?" she responded, but she already knew.

"It's too soon. You're thinking of tonight, and I'm thinking of tomorrow. It'll probably kill me to stop at this point, but this is only a part of the whole picture I'm looking for. It's not the whole picture itself. I want you to clearly see the distinction. Anyway, this was to be a slow wooing, and I apologize."

"For what?" she asked, bewildered and wondering if she'd just been insulted or complimented.

"For rushing you."

"But Greg, I could have stopped you if I'd wanted."

"Nope," he declared empirically, jackknifing off the bed. "You were a goner. I'm going into the other bedroom. I can't handle all this temptation." He leaned over and kissed a soft breast and Andrea shivered. "I'll see you in the morning, love" was all he said as he closed the door behind him.

Andrea flopped back down on her pillow, crossing her arms in exasperation. How about that? He considered her putty in his hands. It was disgusting. It was true. She turned to punch her pillow into submission, then eyed it speculatively. Carefully she turned on her side and pulled the pillow tentatively into her arms. Hmm, the piece of fluff was definitely a second best, she thought, but at this point it was better than nothing. Her final rebellion was to lean way out over the edge of the bed and plug her blanket back in. Then she flicked the control box to high with a flourish of her hand and didn't bother to replace her nightie. It only took her an hour and a half to fall asleep.

She slept a short time, awakening a few hours later, in a sweat. This was a real first, she thought ruefully. Andrea was a blue blood, not by virtue of any impressive ancestry, but rather her own lamentable tendency to shiver during all months but two weeks in mid-July. She was definitely overheated. Again. She threw on her nightgown and left the bedroom. She was startled to find Greg making hot chocolate in the kitchen.

"Couldn't sleep," he mumbled with a shrug. His color rose, and he hoped that Andrea wasn't aware that old medical students could sleep anywhere, even upright, at the slightest excuse. But, he reminded himself, her dad had been a doctor and she might figure out how much peace she had cost him.

"I need a shower," she announced baldly. "Late November, and I'm sweaty. I *never* sweat, no matter how hard I work. Not from the beginning of November until early May. It's strictly a summertime activity for me."

"Women don't sweat anyway."

"You don't spend as much time in a girls' locker room as I do. They not only sweat, they smell when they sweat."

"They don't," he contradicted.

"How do you know? They teach you that in medical school?"

"My mother told me," he answered smugly. "Men sweat, women perspire and ladies glow."

Andrea groaned, "Oh, good heavens above." She hit him with the pillow she was for some reason still clutching. "That's ridiculous."

"Hey!" Greg's muffled protest was all but lost in his efforts to resurface. He knocked the pillow free, grabbed her and found himself staring down the open neckline she had never buttoned. Andrea watched his eyes glaze over as he studied the lightly swathed globes that rose and fell just below the open slash in the yoke. She held her breath, watching the gradual transition and loving the feminine knowledge of her responsibility for it.

He freed one hand to trace a lazy line beginning just beneath one ear, traversing the slim length of her responsive neck, resting temporarily to check a kindling pulse point. His touch then continued down, exploring the shallow valley between her breasts, his finger sliding through the revealing beads of moisture still to be found there.

"Uh, you wouldn't care to retest your mother's theory, would you?" she questioned breathlessly. "See if you can push me past the lady's glow? Sort of like the princess and the pea. Separate the ladies from the women." Her suddenly free hand began a two-fingered walk from his waist and proceeded up his chest. "We could consider earlier a warm-up. Practice."

Greg snapped out of his reverie. "Practice, my rear end. Stop that!" He slapped her hand. "I've created a monster. I'm going back to bed...by myself, mind you, so I can maintain my virtue. I've never accepted second best yet, and I'm not about to start now. I want it all, lady. And I'm going to have it. Now we'll hear no more about practicing tonight, because if you don't can the come-on, you're going to have difficulties waking up tomorrow. I know how you're looking forward to that bird walk.''

Chapter Nine

Dawn came annoyingly early Saturday morning. It brought an equally annoying shoulder-shaking with it.

"Come on, Mary Sunshine. Up and at 'em. Birds are at their most visible first thing in the morning. Rise and shine."

My, but he was disgustingly happy and energetic this morning, she thought. That could easily be chalked up as a point against him.

She mumbled into her pillow and tried to cling to the blankets that Greg was ruthlessly ripping away. "It's too early. The walk doesn't even start until eight..." One of her eyes opened and tried to focus on the bedside clock radio.

"It's only five o'clock. It will not take us three hours to get ready."

"Eight o'clock, pah! They're going to miss everything interesting. Now at six, anything worthwhile will be up scratching around for breakfast. The early bird and all of that."

Andrea crawled out of bed, shaking her head to clear it. One look told her he was serious. She shook her head again, this time in disparagement. "Greg, we can't go without the group. We won't know what we're looking at." She shrugged into her floor-length blue velour robe and lifted the bed skirt to check for her slippers. She needed them. The heat hadn't even kicked on yet, it was so early.

Greg sat on the edge of the bed and began working into a set of thermal-weave long johns, pulling them up under his short robe. He intended to dress in her room, she gathered, because a pile of neatly folded fresh clothes sat on the bed beside him.

"Not to worry. I bought a bird guide the other day at that bookstore on Central Street. Seven ninety-five for the paperback edition. Incredible." He shook his head to show his disbelief.

"I'll start breakfast," she muttered in resignation.

But Greg caught her hand, pulling her between his now jean-clad thighs. "How are you this morning, honey?"

Andrea's eyes wandered, measuring the cracks needing to be plastered on the wall behind him before meeting his gaze in a more straightforward fashion. Her hand awkwardly raked his hair back off his forehead in a nervous gesture. "You were right. We should wait until I'm surer." Her eyes went back to taking inventory of the cracks. "But it would have been an experience."

His arms encircled her hips and he lay his head on her breasts before commenting, "You're sweet and I want you desperately. But I'm afraid it's all or nothing for you and me." He tapped her forehead significantly. "Now tell me what's going on up here. Do I have to protect my flanks from ambush while we're at the nature center? Check over my shoulder all day?"

Andrea laughed. "None of the above. I'm frustrated, but I'll survive."

"I'm glad," he crooned, lifting his head to study her face. "I want you to make that awful health-food milk shake for breakfast that you're so crazy about. When we do start working on our little project, I want you in top form. Little Emmett should get off to the best possible start."

Andrea looked confused. "'Emmett'? Emmett who?"

Greg stood to walk her out to the kitchen. "Emmett is going to be my firstborn son," he informed her seriously. "Heir to one-half of my sterling genetic code. I do not want said code damaged or impaired by poor nutrition on his mother's part." He reached into the box holding everything that had been removed from the dismantled upper cabinets and located the blender. Gravely he handed it to her.

She clutched the blender to her bosom while glaring at him. This was laughable! "How could you possibly be so cruel as to stick a defenseless baby with such a terrible name?"

"There is nothing wrong with that name," he insisted, growing indignant. "I have carried it for thirty years."

"Greg is the diminutive for Gregory, not Emmett. Your name is Gregory. Karen said so."

"My name is Emmett Gregory Rennolds, Jr. My son will be Emmett Gregory Rennolds the third."

Andrea tipped her head and knocked an ear with her palm to clear it. What was she doing at five-fifteen in the morning freezing in a fifty-five degree kitchen, arguing over a fictitious baby's name? "What is it with you? Every time I start thinking we might have a good thing going, you do something like this. If you actually expect some poor woman to spend twenty-odd years cringing every time she has to call her own flesh and blood by name, let me suggest you marry her, get her pregnant and fill in the birth certificate on the sly. *If* I were ever to have a son—" and she stressed the if for his benefit; there was no point in letting him think she had totally buckled under to the spell of his charisma "—he would be christened Emil, after the one-quarter genetic code passed on from his maternal grandfather. I *might* have my arm twisted as far as Gregory Emil, but that's it. You'll have to find some other poor besotted female to sweet-talk into that one. Emmett. What a horrible name."

Greg cracked an egg into the blender and handed her a six-ounce can of frozen concentrated orange juice after pulling the opening strip for her. He almost knew the recipe by heart. "Some other besotted female? Are you admitting to being besotted?"

Andrea peeled a banana, broke it into chunks and tossed them into the blender. The peel was unceremoniously dumped on the top of an overflowing brown grocery bag converted to garbage use. "All I'm saying," she said, avoiding his question, "is that I'm not so far gone that I'd let any son of mine be called Emmett. I'm sorry you got stuck with a rotten name, but I see no reason to perpetuate the crime on future generations. You're going to have to compromise a little, at least on this one issue."

"Emil would be a hundred times worse," Greg returned pugnaciously.

"This is an entirely ludicrous discussion. I am not now, nor will I be in the foreseeable future, pregnant. So why are we standing here arguing over this? The sun's not even up yet, for goodness' sake!" She ended yelling, as if arguments were only allowable during daylight hours.

Greg hushed her and looked meaningfully toward the ceiling. "You'll wake them, and Karen needs her rest."

Andrea merely stared at him for a significantly lengthy period of time. Finally she shoved a glass of the finished breakfast concoction into his hand and advised, "Here, drink this. And by the way, you'll have to take the garbage out before we go. I'd do it, but my shoes have disappeared again."

Greg tossed the drink down in one long, shuddering motion. It was the only way he could stomach the stuff. "They're by the back door. Remember, you stepped on that piece of ice, only it wasn't totally frozen and your shoes sank in the water? You didn't want to track through the house."

"Oh, that's right. I forgot. I don't suppose you know where my keys are?" She arched a hopeful eyebrow in his direction.

"Try your purse. I seem to remember being amazed to see you actually putting them where they belonged."

Andrea brightened. "Thanks. I never would have thought of looking there."

"I've said it before, you need a keeper," Greg grunted in mock despair as he deftly hefted the heavy garbage bag into the crook of his left arm. "I'll meet you at the car. Bring the green plastic bag off my dresser, would you? I bought two pairs of 7 x 35 mm binoculars the other day."

"Am I supposed to be impressed?"

He shrugged his shoulders. "Beats me. It's what the bird book suggested."

"Where is this infamous bird book? You may as well bring it along since we're actually going to go through with this."

The two hours before the guided tour of the nature center began served only to impress upon Andrea how basically incompatible she and Greg were. True, Greg had been correct in that there were a lot of birds up and about. Unfortunately, to the uninitiated, they all looked alike.

"What's that?" she inquired while shading her eyes from the early-morning glare with a hand. She pointed to a preening bird strutting on a low branch fifteen feet over their heads.

Greg looked in the general direction of her wavering forefinger. "Where? I don't see anything."

Andrea pointed more emphatically. "Right there. Just follow my finger and look." She wondered if bird dogs had as much difficulty pointing out their prey to their hunting partners.

"I still don't...oh. That? Let's see..." Greg began industriously flipping through his book. "First thing to do is determine its size. Robins are the measuring stick you go buy. So, is it bigger or smaller than a robin?"

"I don't know. I don't see one around to compare it with." Her eyes turned in a slow, searching arc. "I think they all went south already."

Greg exhaled an exasperated sigh. "Lots of robins stay all winter. You only notice them in the spring because you're looking for them. It's a fallacy that they're the first sign of spring. But that's all beside the point. I'm sure they don't mean exact micrometer comparisons. Generally speaking, is that bird roughly the same size as, smaller than, or larger than a robin?"

"Oh, well, if that's the case... my guess is, maybe a little smaller. What do you think?"

He ignored her query and turned back to his guide. "Fine. Smaller. Now what are its distinguishing characteristics, starting with the markings around the eyes?"

This was starting to resemble the Grand Inquisition. How the devil was she supposed to see its eyes from this distance? "I can't see that far."

"That's what the field glasses are for," Greg pointed out in false equanimity.

"Right," she mumbled while raising the forgotten glasses to her eyes for a closer look. She lowered them to take a new fix on the bird before elevating them again. Then she tried a third time to no avail. She simply could not find the stupid thing when looking through the binoculars.

"Oh, hell. Give me the damn glasses," Greg rumbled in disgust, strangling her with the neck strap as he tugged the glasses away.

"Hey!" she gasped indignantly. "Use your own!"

Dropping hers with a snort and picking up the pair hanging forlornly around his own neck, he instructed in short tones, "Look, you keep your eyes on the bird while you raise the binoculars to your face. The glasses have a much narrower field of vision than your eyes, and you'll never find it otherwise. Hell, where is the thing?"

"I think it just flew away."

He turned to her, an annoyed furrow deepening in his creased brow. "Did you notice anything at all about it?"

Helpfully, she offered, "It was kind of brown. Yes, a mottled brown, with some white."

Greg crouched, not wanting to sit in the nature center's six-inch layering of composting damp brown leaves and pine needles. He showed her several silhouettes and full-color pictures of various birds with a quick thrusting jab of an index finger. "Was his profile like this? Did he hold his tail up or let it drop like here? What about this one? It's kind of mottled brown."

She tried not to get nauseated from the rapidly flipping pages of color wavering in front of her eyes. How was she to differentiate between so many brown birds? There must be twenty or thirty, all sporting variegated tones of brown. "Greg, I really didn't see it all that well. Maybe we'd better just forget that one and hope for better luck next time. Surely they won't all fly away so fast...."

Greg rose from his crouch and impatiently remonstrated, "You're going to have to get the characteristic markings more quickly, that's all. No bird is going to sit still for twenty to thirty minutes while you catalog its each and every feature."

Andrea was cut to the quick. She placed both hands on her hips and glared. "You've got binoculars. Why don't you see how quickly *you* can identify them?"

"I can't do it all," he snapped back in aggrieved tones. "One of the keys to success is delegating and cooperating. In this case, that translates to you spot 'em and I'll find 'em in the book."

"You make it sound so easy," Andrea snorted as she stomped off. Stopping again, she pointed to a fence some fifty feet in the distance. "There's one."

Squinting in the proper direction, Greg made a disgusted sound. "That's a pigeon, for heaven's sake."

"So what's wrong with pigeons?" Andrea demanded.

"Nothing's wrong with pigeons. They're a dime a dozen, that's all. I was hoping for something a little more unusual."

By the time the professional guide arrived, they had spotted a crow, a mallard duck and two more mottled-brown, smaller-than-a-robin birds that wouldn't sit still long enough to be identified. And Greg and Andrea were barely speaking to each other.

Greg drove home with a white-knuckled grip on the steering wheel. He was the first one away from any intersection where a red light dared stop them, no contest. Andrea breathed a sigh of relief when he finally pulled to a stop in front of her own little bungalow. They found Karen and Tim in the kitchen.

"So how'd it go?" Karen queried from her position on the floor where she sat trying to organize the boxes of foods removed from the cabinets into some semblance of usable order.

Greg rolled his eyes. "Don't ask." He left for his room telling Tim to wait a minute and he'd help him mount the new cabinet he was working with onto the wall.

"What's with Prince Charming?" Tim wagged his head at Greg's departing back. "Birding wasn't quite the fun-filled outing he had in mind?"

"Once we had someone who knew what they were doing with us, it was fine. She helped us identify two cardinals, male and female, a yellow-shafted flicker, the biggest blue jay I've ever seen and nine sparrows—seven house and two white-throated. Those are kind of brown mottled birds, a little smaller than robins with some white on them. It was fun. Much to my surprise, I actually enjoyed myself." Her index finger paused reflectively against her lower lip. "I don't think Greg had a very good time, though. I think he was expecting something a little more exotic. The lady explained that we were fortunate to live on one of America's four great migratory paths, the Mississippi flyway. Evidently, during the fall and spring migrations, there are a lot of unusual specimens coming through. Unfortunately, Greg's taken up the hobby a month too late and most of the unusual ones have already come and gone." Andrea shrugged. "Now he has to wait until May."

Karen chuckled, "That must be driving him crazy. He never was too good at goal postponement."

"I've noticed," Andrea returned dryly, thinking of their own relationship, but the remark went over Karen's head.

Tim interceded. "Listen, Andrea, if he's going to sulk in his room much longer, maybe you'd better help me. I need someone to hold the level while I position this cabinet and tell me when I've got it right."

"Sorry, *mon cher*." Andrea carelessly waltzed her way to the doorway connecting the dining room and kitchen. "I'm working in here today. Let the Credit Prince help you, they belong to him anyway. I didn't want the darn cabinets in the first place."

"Andrea," Tim retorted, "you're being a trifle small about all of this. He was thinking of you."

She had intended to go blithely on her way, but that stung. "Just as I'm sure my father's buy-now, pay-later purchases were all intended to benefit my mother. No, thank you. I don't need that kind of devotion."

Tim wasn't finished with her, though. Not yet. It was time for her to put another aspect of her childhood into perspective, ready or not.

"Listen here, young lady," he said, sounding paternal. "Have you ever stopped to think about how much rental apartments go for these days? You looked for him. You should know. Then put food, utilities and laundry on top of that. Now think of the small sum he pays you for the room and all those services. You've made it possible for him to well afford a hefty monthly payment on the furniture he bought the other day and these cabinets and *still* come out smelling like a rose. It's time you stopped trying to push him into your father's mold. Greg's a far cry from going down the tubes yet. Now get the level, would you?"

Andrea looked at him a little uncertainly. He had a knack for making her seem petty when he discussed her differences with Greg. Sighing, she capitulated. "All right, all right. Where is it?"

"It's on top of the refrigerator, and stop looking like Saint Joan at the stake. I'm sorry to have to yell at you, but someone has to make you see reason. He loves you. You love him. It's elemental. Stop building complications into it."

"I said 'all right,' didn't I?" She retrieved the tool and plopped it on the cabinet Tim was propping into place. Leaning over, she squinted. "The bubble's off to the right...oops, too much, back a little the other way...almost, just a hair... There."

"Great," Tim grunted. "Draw a line on the wall across the top so I can put it down and start some screw holes into the studs."

"Well, hurry it up," Andrea grumbled as she followed his instructions. "I want to make some hot chocolate. I can't seem to get warm after being outside all morning."

Tim quirked an inquisitive eyebrow in her direction. "For as long as I've known you, you've frozen all winter, every winter. Why don't you break down and turn up the heat?"

Andrea gave an inelegant snort and turned away. Always cold, hah! Not anymore. He should have seen her last night!

Greg came back into the room seemingly in an improved frame of mind. He and Tim began to battle with the new cabinets while Andrea hovered over the hot pot where she warmed her hands as well as the water for hot chocolate.

Work progressed quickly until an hour or two after a slapdash cold-cuts lunch. Karen sorted the spices, throwing out anything more than a year out of code and munching on a cache of Oreos she'd found. Andrea went back and forth between Greg and Tim, proclaiming cabinets level, fetching assorted drill bits and screws, and providing slivers of wood with which cabinets were shimmied. Her head buzzed, but just being in Greg's presence had a way of doing that to her. However, gradually it began to ache with an intensity that threatened to virtually incapacitate her. She gave in to the inevitable when Tim, who stood three steps up on the ladder, kept missing the screwdriver she was holding up to his back and finally turned to see where she was.

"My God, Andrea, you're as pale as can be. Why didn't you say something? You're sick, aren't you? Go to bed. We'll manage without you."

Karen looked up from her rolls of unwound shelf paper and set her scissors down. "You look awful," she concurred. "I'll plug in the hot pot again and bring you in a cup of tea. Go tuck yourself in and put the blanket on high. I'll try to find a thermometer for you once I get the water going."

"It really isn't necessary, Karen. Don't go to all that bother. I'll be fine. Really." *Oh, my.* She shouldn't have shaken her head no like that, she realized, because the room was definitely spinning. And she wasn't going to talk anymore, either. Her voice was reverberating around the inside of her head like a drumroll in an echo chamber.

Greg had been consumed with wrestling another cabinet in through the back door when Karen led Andrea from the room. At first he'd noticed nothing suspicious, as Karen had come back and put on more water for tea; she and Andrea often had tea in the afternoon. But when he observed her putting the small pot on a tray along with a mug and disappearing into Andrea's room, it clicked: Something was wrong.

Karen almost dumped the boiling pot into Andrea's lap when Greg came bursting through the door demanding, "What's going on? What's wrong with Andrea?"

"Nothing is wrong with Andrea," Andrea mumbled through pain-stiffened lips. "Other than the fact that I'm dying, everything is just fine. Now go away. I'm not up to entertaining at the moment." She closed her rapidly glazing eyes and concentrated on not hyperventilating.

Greg took her at her word and began a one-man crusade to stave off her dire fate. "Karen, go get my bag out of my room. And hurry up about it, will you? She looks awful." He raked an exasperated hand through his sawdust-powdered hair, stopping when he only succeeded in inflicting pain as his fingers caught in the tight curls. "I don't understand it. You seemed fine earlier on our walk. What is it, your stomach? Your head? Do you still have your appendix? Maybe I ought to take you to the emergency room. Is your hospitalization any good?" Turning to Karen in irritation as he noticed her still gawking at the end of the bed, he spoke harshly. "Where is my bag? What are you waiting for, Christmas?"

"Greg," Karen said in amazement. "If this is an example of your bedside manner, I think you ought to reconsider your vocation in life. A doctor can't afford to fall apart every time somebody gets a little ache or pain."

"Can we go into your analysis of my career choice later on? Just get the bag." He studied Andrea's pale countenance. "'Little ache,' my foot. It's probably double pneumonia. Maybe strep throat." He picked up her hand and patted it solicitously. "I wonder where we could get a culture done without having to wait at the hospital."

Andrea shook her head in despair and was again immediately sorry as the room went into a tailspin. He was talking about hospitals, infected lungs and throat cultures. But he had yet to even ask what part of her body actually hurt. "Greg," she informed him, "I just have a headache. I'm probably catching a cold or the flu. There's no need to get so excited. I'm just going to lie down for a while, and I'll be fine. Scout's honor."

"I take it all back, Andrea," Karen advised as she came back into the room. "You were right, but for the wrong reasons. If you marry him, he'll drive you crazy every time you sneeze. This must be why doctors don't treat their own families. They fall apart at the seams when it's one of their own."

That got Andrea's attention. *Is that why he was so upset? Was she really one of his own?*

Greg paid Karen no heed, his attention totally on Andrea's suffering visage. He popped open his bag and stared in disgust at its limited contents. He could listen to her heart and lungs. That was about it. "Sit up a little, honey. I want to listen at your back."

Honey. He had called her honey. Wasn't that the sweetest thing? Even though Greg was bellowing around the room like a wounded buffalo, making her head clang like the largest bell in the church belfry, it suddenly all struck her as rather...sweet. Boy, she must really be sicker than she thought.

Greg took her temperature and found it slightly raised. "Do you have any aspirin substitute?"

She held her head to still the echoing his booming voice had caused and whispered through gritted teeth, "You bought some last night, remember? But I'm not going to take it unless this gets a whole lot worse. All that stuff nauseates me."

Greg stared at her in open astonishment. It was clear he thought she had more than one loose screw in her brain. "This is ridiculous," Greg spoke indignantly. "You're virtually incapacitated, and we should try to get your temperature down."

"It's not all that high, Greg. And it seems to me a clearcut case of the cure being worse than the disease. I told you. The pills make me throw up and my temperature's not that bad. If you would just let me sleep it off, I'm sure I'd be okay in no time."

He felt her head one more time, possibly for luck, she suspected. His calm, more collected medical demeanor was rapidly slipping into place now that his sense of emergency was fading.

"Well, I suppose you know your own body."

She should hope she did. But he still looked doubtful as he pulled the covers up to her chin and kissed her pain-puckered forehead.

"Stay in bed and try to sleep. When I'm done with Tim, I'll make a can of bean-and-bacon soup and some popcorn for dinner. It's not gourmet, but it'll be filling. Call if you want Karen to make a fresh pot of tea."

Andrea's appalled voice stopped his exit. "Popcorn and beans for dinner?" How could anyone face such a prospect? Her weakened condition certainly precluded even the mere thought.

Gently he chided her. "Surely you know popcorn and baked beans are incomplete proteins that complement each other perfectly. Like red beans and rice. Buck up. It won't be so bad." There seemed to be a slightly sadistic gleam in his eye as he continued. "Besides, I thought you'd be ecstatic to see me using soup in the menu."

With amazing agility for a man his size, he was through the door and had it closed before she could manufacture an effective retort.

Andrea's headache proved to be not much more than that. Work on the house progressed nicely as winter slowly lost its grip on Chicago. December, January and February passed in breath-fogging tones of gray. The kitchen was finished and gorgeous. The old Formica table had been replaced with a work island/breakfast bar complete with an indoor grill. Karen's stomach had assumed astonishing proportions. The dining room sported lush paper on its walls and magnificent pecan-tone cabinets in its corners. Tim was only a few weeks short of his law degree and had three job offers with good, reliable—although not LaSalle Street—firms. Tim informed them that all those fancy downtown firms weren't ready for his brilliance anyhow, and he'd give them a few more years to prepare his office suite before tackling that bastion of high-powered partnerships.

Greg was the only fly in the ointment. He had spent December and January working on Andrea along with the house. He had taken up unofficial residency in Karen and Tim's vacated first-floor bedroom. And for those two months he had seemed firmly entrenched. Even his sister Loretta had stopped calling and Andrea was sure she was suspected of sorcery.

Things had begun to fall apart in February. Greg's personality dictated action on knotty problems. That trait of his was in direct conflict with Andrea's cautious approach to life. He saw no progress in their stand-off. She felt like a penniless orphan in front of a candy-store window display. My, how she wanted it, but she was afraid she didn't have or even truly know the price.

Greg's practice blossomed. Andrea was eaten up with jealousy each time the phone rang. How could so many honey-voiced women's bodies all malfunction at the same time? Sometimes at night she dreamed of them crawling out of the bungalow's woodwork and sliding into the bed just down the hall, comforting Greg while she shivered in her solitary bed with nothing but knee socks, flannel gown and robe, and an electric blanket. Andrea just knew it was only a matter of time before Greg forgot whatever it had been that had attracted him to her in the first place and took up with one of the mellow-sounding sweethearts on the other end of the phone wire. She was cynical enough to suspect they weren't all flocking to his office just for his medical skills. *Heck no!* They had eyes, just as she did.

Greg spent early February harassing her unmercifully. He had an uncanny ability to zero in on her weakest spot and worry at it like a dog with a bone. First there were her middle-class mores and the old double standard. What if the school found out she was living with a man? What would the parents say? What would *her* parents say? Definitely hitting below the belt.

It was the last week in February before Greg, tenacious to the end, finally admitted defeat. The confrontation took place in the kitchen, where so many of their confrontations had. Pots were tossed about and scrubbed with enough vigor to remove their aluminum coating along with the grease. Andrea suspected he would have gladly substituted her neck, given the opportunity.

Was she or was she not going to marry him in the foreseeable future?

She just wasn't ready to make that commitment quite yet.

Had he or had he not given her over three months to think about things since he had gotten serious?

He had indeed.

Did she or did she not love him?

She suspected she did.

Did she believe he loved her?

She wanted to...

He threw up his hands in disgust, soapsuds flying in all directions. They spattered on the floor, on the clean drying kettles and on Andrea herself. That had done it. He gave up. Nothing he did convinced her of his love. Not his lack of dates—and he'd had plenty of opportunities—not all the work he had put in on her house when he should have been concentrating on building up his practice, nor his patience in waiting for her to come around, nothing.

Greg fixed her with a narrow-eyed stare. "I've found a nice apartment between Northwestern University and the hospital. I'm going to sign the lease tomorrow and move this weekend. It's available the first, which is Thursday, but I'm too busy to shop for a bed and such until Saturday."

Andrea literally wrung her hands. Just when she'd finally gotten used to him being around, he was going to take his marbles and go home. Well, she'd always known he would. That was why she hadn't wanted to make a commitment, wasn't it? But Saturday was only five days away! And good grief, the bungalow was almost as much his as hers at this point.

"What about the cabinets?" she asked. "And the dining-room furniture you bought? The Murphy bed we're refinishing down in the basement?" She looked at everything around her, bewildered. Without Greg, the place would be almost personality-less. Heavens, she still had the Golden Gate Bridge in her garage, just waiting for a warm spring day to be set up in the backyard. Even though she'd known this was coming, it was still catching her by surprise somehow.

"Keep 'em," he said disgustedly. "They're only things, Andrea. They can't keep you warm at night the way I could have."

"But...but they were so expensive..."

Again he snorted in derision. "When are you going to get over your money hang-ups? Money buys *things*. That's all it's good for. Big deal. And money certainly can't buy me what I really want...your love...now can it? So what good does it do me?"

When she just stared at him, he threw the dish towel he had been drying his hands with down on the cabinets and left the room with what sounded an awful lot like a snarl....

Tuesday, Wednesday and Thursday evenings he had watched her, following her every move until she felt ready to break apart. What was he looking for? She actually felt like porcelain. One good bump, and she would shatter. And late that night, in the bed heated only by electricity, she worked to bring herself back under control. If tomorrow night was to be their last together, she wanted to remember it with pleasure. The end of a cherishing time. Sleep came with the determination to have as normal a day as possible followed by as warm an evening as possible. She would not crack.

And then it was morning. Andrea sat on one of her new breakfast stools and bemusedly gazed across the breakfast bar. She looked past Greg's dark head, which was bent over the *Tribune*'s sports section, and stared out the recently installed triple-glazed window. Absently she cradled her breakfast milk shake and wondered if it would actually reach the predicted seventy-one degrees. It was only March 2 and Chicago winters never gave up that easily. It had to be a trick of some sort.

Andrea rose and rinsed her glass in the sink. Turning back to Greg's engrossed face, she enquired, "Do you want a cup of coffee before I go?" The thought of leaving didn't seem to be breaking him apart, she thought a little resentfully. He seemed as relaxed and calm as could be.

The sound of her voice broke the early-morning quiet and Greg glanced up with a start. "What? Oh, no, I guess not. This is fine, thanks." He indicated his own glass containing the dregs of his breakfast drink with a wave of his hand and frowned. "It says here they may not be able to have Wrigley Field ready for the Cubs opener. All the snow we've had has kept them from working on the field. It's been too muddy since the snow's melted and now there's more snow expected when the cool front comes through later on today."

"That's too bad," Andrea responded, sounding almost sincere. *Who the heck cared?* How could he discuss baseball at a time like this? Well, if he could forget the morning's real significance, so could she.

She forced her thoughts into returning to more practical matters. Maybe if the warm weather was only due to last a day, she'd better figure out something to do with the girls outside. Early spring fever would be a foregone conclusion on a day like today. The parking lot should be dry enough to use if the field wasn't.

Again she glanced at Greg's closely cropped mahogany curls as she kissed him and readied herself to leave. She loved him, she acknowledged. But she hadn't been able to bring herself to the point of commitment and babies yet. She wanted to, at least on an intellectual plane, and she hoped Greg understood that. A while back, he had said he would wait for her to come to him, to tell him when she had successfully cleared all the hurdles. But she suspected that tomorrow's move signified the end of his patience.

Andrea felt petty and small as she absently patted a hand along the kitchen windowsill, searching for her car keys. What was wrong with her that she couldn't trust in his love enough to take that final step? She was managing to open up enough on other fronts. There had been a serious money discussion late one night in front of a fireplace so hot, the flames burned with a blue light. Of course, that had been when Greg had talked in terms of "us" and "ours." Now she guessed that it was back to "me" and "you."

He had been ill at ease that night, and she had known why as soon as he blurted out, "Andrea, I'd like to see you mortgage the house."

She had forced herself to remain pliant in his arms, but internally her stomach had twisted into knots. Her mind had raced in two conflicting directions at once. This was the man she purported to love. Love without trust was nothing. But a mortgage on her hard-won clear title? Oh, no.

"If you'll study the tax laws, you'll see that it makes a great deal of sense for a person in our tax bracket to have a mortgage. Not only can you deduct the interest off the income tax, but you could use the capital freed to invest in tax-free investments, like a retirement savings plan or something. Especially once we're married and filing jointly, we'll end up saving a lot in the long run. I'd like to show you some facts and figures if you'll let me." He'd treated their marriage as a foregone conclusion back then.

Rationally, Andrea had known that what he was saying made sense, but emotionally...oh, no. Her house. His wary posture exuded defensiveness and she'd wondered if her own anxieties were as easily read. It was hard, but she had forced herself to follow her new line of trust. "No, I don't want to see any facts or figures, Greg." Then she hurried to allay his clear disappointment. "No, it's not that. It's just, well...I trust you in this. If you feel that's the proper way to handle the available funds, then I'll do it." Poking fun at her own cold feet, she wryly added, "Don't take it wrong if I keep a little that's easily liquidated, okay? Just in case I revert to my usual chicken behavior and decide to run."

Collapsing on top of her, Greg had ruffled his hands through her hair and leered menacingly, "It's too late now, baby. You couldn't run fast enough. You'll never get away from me."

The soft pile of the area rug had tickled the nape of her neck as he had proceeded to demonstrate the extent of her captivity. Holding her hands over her head in one of his own, he had let the other roam the slender length of her neck and down over the gentle curves of her breasts. Her shirt had been easily pulled up and out of the way, and he had bent to kiss the trembling tips of the small uncovered mounds.

"Oh, Andrea," he had breathed as she arched helplessly underneath him. "You've come so far. There's such a little distance left. Hurry, love. I'm a glutton. I want everything. I'm waiting for the day you come to me freely, trusting in me and my love. Give me the gift of all of you, and not just the inconsequential things. On that day you won't be able to keep me out of your bed and we'll start a loving worth something and a marriage worth sharing." His head had dipped, allowing his tongue to torment the shallow well of her navel. "It's so hard to be patient. Don't make me wait forever. Come to me soon."

Her stomach had trembled against the slight force of his breathy plea. "I'm trying, Greg," she'd whispered in return, craving his touch and no longer surprised by that knowledge.

"It would be good between us, Andrea. I know it."

"Would it, Greg? I've taught all the facts...but I never...this is...different than I expected."

"And this is just the tip of the iceberg, sweetheart. You and I, we could have it all, if only you'll let us." She was never really sure if she heard him, since they'd drifted off in front of the fire soon after, but he'd never mentioned it again in such a serious vein. Instead, he had teased her and watched with hot, hungry eyes that spoke of his impatience. But his waiting was over now. He was calling the game. Her side had defaulted, and he'd be out looking for a more willing partner after tomorrow.

Andrea's thoughts were cut off as she frowned at the empty windowsill. "Greg, do you know..."

Reaching around to the countertop behind him, Greg's hand disappeared between two of her new harvest-gold Tupperware canisters, reappearing a moment later, the missing keys dangling from a crooked finger. His eyes never leaving the paper, he informed her in preoccupied tones, "Your shoes are under the radiator in the bathroom."

"They are? How'd they get there? Never mind. Thanks." He was obviously too engrossed in the continuing saga of the mayor versus the city council to be paying much attention to the migratory patterns of her running shoes. She retrieved them and left. The promise of a beautiful day was somehow spoiled by her self-acknowledged failure to take that final step in trust.

Chapter Ten

The cold front arrived halfway through seventh period. Thankfully, that was Andrea's last teaching class of the day. She herded the girls in to shower in preparation for their biology class and wondered why she bothered. The addition of a little honest sweat could not possibly worsen the odor of the formaldehyde-soaked fetal pigs being dissected in that wing of the school.

She watched as the mercury plummeted. Forty-two degrees in forty-five minutes, until it hovered just below freezing. Lead-gray clouds blanketed the sky in foreboding until they finally severed earth from the last persistent ray escaping the sun's ball of orange.

Andrea left the school building just about then and edged her yellow car out from between a colleague's battered station wagon and a visiting parent's shiny sedan. Anxiously she glanced skyward as the first fat flakes drifted down in aimless abandon. She'd better stop at the grocery. These were typical Chicago blizzard conditions. The clash of a retreating warm front and militant cool front mixed with the possibility of lake-effect snow and barely freezing temperatures could easily combine to spell big trouble. She watched a flake settle on the windshield, not fooled by the wiper's momentary success in dealing with it. These were fat, lacy flakes. Anyone knew big fat ones mounted up much faster than the little pellet kind. What's more, Chicago was ripe for a blizzard. There hadn't been more than five or six inches of snow on the ground at any one time in the past two winters.

Just to be safe, five days' worth of groceries were loaded into the rear of the car. She had bought two gallons of milk. There was something about having milk in the house when you were snowed in and cut off from the world that lent a sense of security, even if you never drank the stuff. But they would drink it, she assured herself self-righteously. There was Karen to think of. Pregnant women needed lots of milk. Otherwise the baby would take the calcium from the mother and Karen's teeth would rot. She went back and got a third gallon.

There were two inches of snow on the ground by the time she slid down the alley and parked the car safely in the ramshackle garage. She eyed it critically as she went around to the back of the car to retrieve the groceries. The garage would have to be next on the list. With her luck, she'd find the weight of some new snow collapsing the roof of the thing on her meticulously polished car if she didn't remodel it by next winter.

Dropping her keys and purse into the top of the nearest bag, she grabbed that one and its neighbor and began lugging them up to the house. "Hi," she said brightly to Karen, who had seen her struggling and was holding the back door open. "Have you listened to the weather at all? What are they predicting?"

Karen eyed the groceries suspiciously. "What'd you do? Buy out the store?"

Andrea ignored her condescending tone. She hadn't bought anything they wouldn't eventually use. She just wouldn't have to go to the store for a while, that was all. She set the sacks on the countertop and paused to catch her breath before going back for the rest. "Better to be safe," she puffed dismissively. "What're they saying? I missed it on the car radio while I was in the store."

Karen looked at her in pitying superiority. "The way you overreact to a few snowflakes, one would think you must have been snowed in for a month with no food or supplies at an early, impressionable age." Shaking her head in mock disparagement, she enlightened her. "We're only due for four to six inches, a little more by the lake. Since it's Friday and they're expecting temperatures around thirty-five to forty all weekend, there'll be no problems by rush hour Monday morning. You see?" she questioned rhetorically to Andrea's retreating back as she left to carry in the rest of her purchases. "You've done it again. It's March, for crying out loud. What did you expect? Oh, my Lord. Three gallons of milk?"

By six o'clock at least four inches of snow had fallen, the beauty of its whiteness lost in the increasingly hazardous swirls of thick flakes. Andrea hummed around the stove, checking the simmering stew and adding a can of cream of mushroom to thicken its gravy. She covered her bread dough and set it out to rise. There was something about the weather that brought out the pioneer spirit in her and demanded a bit of bread-baking.

Greg came out of the bathroom freshly attired in clean though threadbare jeans, loose sweatshirt and no shoes. If only those swooning women patients of his could see him now. She looked at him critically. They'd still swoon. He looked darn good, even in faded blue jeans and worn socks with holes in the heels.

He noticed the four place settings as he passed the open dining-room French doors. "Karen and Tim coming down tonight?" The closely knit group still ate supper together several times a week.

Andrea nodded in affirmation. "I don't think they're going to stay very long, though. Karen cleaned their apartment from one end to the other for some reason, and she's pretty tired. She wants to go to bed early."

Greg chuckled in appreciation. "I know how she feels. I've been up since that phone call at one this morning. I'm dead on my feet." He stretched and yawned in a visual demonstration of the extent of his fatigue. "But if she does that again closer to the end of the month, make her stop. She should start conserving her energy. A lot of women get that last burst of energy and use it up housecleaning instead of recognizing it as a sign of impending delivery and saving it up for the long haul of labor. Keep your eye on her," he instructed, before finally stopping the fascinating display of stretching his muscles.

"Roger. Will do." Andrea saluted in acknowledgement of his order. Then, because she didn't want to dwell on the time coming when he wouldn't be there to stop her himself, she asked, "How was the delivery last night? I didn't think to ask this morning."

"Not bad, just long. They only called me in so early in the labor because the husband was falling apart and had his poor wife half crazy. She couldn't keep herself under control and take care of him, too. It happens some times." He shrugged dismissively. "Especially when the man refuses to properly prepare himself and go to childbirth classes. I finally had to ask him to leave the room. He had absolutely no idea what to expect and certainly wasn't expecting what he got."

Andrea looked at him in wide-eyed astonishment. "Wasn't the wife angry with you?"

"Actually, she was relieved. Without his fussing and fuming we got her back to proper breathing techniques, and she was fine. She said it served him right. It'll be a good long time before he's back in her good graces, I suspect. He missed one of the peak emotional highs of his marriage through his own damn fault." He wagged his head in disbelief at the man's evident stupidity.

Thoughtfully Andrea stirred the stew, this time adding a cup of sour cream and a healthy slug of red wine to the broth before turning off the flame and reaching for a hot pad to rescue the browning biscuits from the oven. She didn't hear Greg's approach until his arms encircled her. His hands caressed her flat belly while his lips moistly nibbled her neck, burrowing provocatively beneath the silky lengths of black hair.

"I helped that baby into the world, and all I could think of was how much I wished you could have trusted in my love."

Andrea found it grating the way he was speaking in the past tense now.

"I'd have had a tough time keeping my hands to myself if you were swollen with our child," he advised. "And if you were laboring to give birth, no force on this earth would have been strong enough to pull me from your side." His hands came gliding up to cup her rapidly swelling breasts in their strong, capable grasp. As he applied an aching, wonderfully firm pressure to them, he whispered in her ear, and his warm breath made her shiver as it gently gusted against her soft cheek. "After the baby's born, the father—that would have been me—cuts the cord, making the child his own person, his own entity. They hand him to the mother—that would have been you—and I'd have helped you put him to your breast. God, Andrea, you have no idea what a special moment that is—the intense emotional bonding I have seen between a husband and wife in the delivery room. Grown men weeping, supercilious little smiles plastered ear to ear, they're so moved by the miracle of life before them."

Surreptitiously, he wiped a glistening eye before reclaiming her breast and gently pressing her to lean back against him. "I fully intend to do my share of eye wiping when my time comes," he said. "I'll admit I've come damn close just watching other couples."

Andrea turned in his arms, locking her own arms around the back of his neck. She was filled with the wonder of Greg's harshly whispered words and his total ease with his own manliness that he could confess to an ability to not only cry, but to anticipate with pleasure a time when he would do it in public, his emotions raw and open for all to see. With each new insight he gave into himself, he made her love for him deepen further, as it did at that moment. Inside her, the fear of losing her chance of sharing a life with him was beginning to balance with the worry of jumping into a marriage without being certain.

There was an unspoken agreement that dinner was to be a lighthearted affair. Frequent trips to the window confirmed the radio's observation that the storm center had stalled over the city, the heavily laden lead clouds intent on dumping their entire contents before moving on. Twelve inches of snow lay on the ground by ten o'clock and it was falling so thickly that anything standing more than two feet outside the windowpane was lost in the intense whiteout. Andrea's spirits rose as the drifts grew. There was no way Greg was going to be able to move this weekend, and he was too busy at work to do so during the week. She might get another whole week of Greg in her life as a result of this ridiculous March blizzard.

After dinner the room's four occupants lounged in front of a determined fire that crackled and spit in an effort to rid itself of the moisture and snow clinging to its newly fetched log offerings. There was no need to panic; Andrea had bought enough groceries for several days. It being March, streets would be plowed or the snow melted to an easily accessible level within a day or two. Greg had no imminent deliveries of his own and he was not on call for the other doctors this weekend. He must realize that his move would have to be delayed, but he didn't seem unduly upset. And there was no other reason not to enjoy the novelty of being snowed in so late in the year.

Karen lay on the floor doing exercises designed to ease the pressure in the small of her back. It seemed to help. "Good thing the baby's not due for close to three weeks," she huffed. "Be just my luck to deliver in a blizzard."

Greg carelessly agreed. "Yep. I'm glad I'm not on call. Anyone due anytime soon is probably in labor right about now. Severe changes in the barometric pressure like we've had today tend to get things moving. Full moon, too, according to some people, and we've got both tonight."

"You're kidding."

"God's truth." Greg drew a pious cross over his heart. "Cross my heart and hope to die." He sat up, supporting himself on his forearms, and Andrea knew they were in for a lecture pulled from his fund of trivia. "We tend to forget man's affinity with the elements as civilization gets more and more sophisticated, taking us further and further from nature by creating these unnatural climates... warmth from central heating in the winter, air-conditioned cool in summer." He seemed to realize he was starting to lose track of his topic and gathered himself into an upright, seated posture to make a better presentation. "As I said, we've lost sight of the close affinity man and nature originally operated under. All kinds of things affected man. Tides, full moons, whatever..." He waved his hand in a distracted gesture. "They all affected us, even down to regulating our sex drive. Still do to some extent, in fact."

Karen and Andrea both gasped a simultaneous *"What?"*

Greg was not to be swayed. "No, really. For example, Karen, didn't you tell me your baby was due toward the end of the month?"

Karen eyed him suspiciously and answered slowly, "I'm due the twenty-first."

"Ah, the twenty-first of March. Couldn't be better. How terribly primitive of you two."

Tim looked intrigued. Curiously, he asked, "Why's that?"

"I just know you shouldn't have asked," Karen groaned.

Greg was thoroughly warmed to his topic now and ignored Karen in favor of answering Tim. "Primitive man, naturally enough, spent a lot of his time outdoors. Now," he quizzed Karen, "when is the longest day of the year? The day man would be exposed to the most sunshine?"

"Anybody knows that," Karen groused. "The summer solstice. When is it, the twentieth or twenty-first of June?"

Greg congratulated her with a brilliant smile, quite taking Andrea's breath away. That smile could belong to her.

"Right. Now a woman getting pregnant around then would carry through the summer, fall and winter. She'd deliver nine months later, right around the spring equinox, sometime during the last half of March or so."

Tim looked puzzled. "So?"

"So," Greg explained. "A baby born at that time of the year would have six full months of decent weather, possibly more, to grow and mature before the hard winter months set in, giving him a much better chance of survival."

In spite of herself, Andrea broke in, "You're going to tell us that the tides are high in the middle of June, right? And they drove early man into a sexual frenzy, causing him to impregnate any female within his range."

Greg frowned in her direction. "Not very likely."

"Okay, I give up. What got to him around the solstice that provided for all those springtime births?" Karen ungraciously questioned, finally giving in to her curiosity.

"Pay attention, now," Greg instructed. "This is good. There's a gland at the base of your throat. It's very light sensitive and," he paused dramatically, "one of the hormones it manufactures is a sexual stimulant. Being light sensitive, it works overtime during the month of June when the days are the longest, putting primitive man's libido into overdrive and thereby ensuring lots of early-spring babies." He sat back, looking highly pleased with himself.

Tim only looked puzzled. "But if this gland is on the inside, how does the light get to it to sensitize it?"

"Skin is translucent, not opaque. Filtered light does get through, especially in a narrow area such as the throat."

Andrea was rather intrigued by the entire discussion. "And here I thought baby booms were caused by electrical blackouts."

Greg and Karen laughed and Tim observed. "Huh. I happen to know they're caused by...ouch!" He rubbed the rib Karen had reached with her kick and gave her a wounded look. She didn't look the least penitent, having given up her back presses to deliver the blow.

"They don't want to hear your theories, Tim, dear," she advised sweetly. "Let them use their imagination, why don't you?"

For such a sweet little thing, she had a way of getting her point across. "Uh, sure. Well, anyway, here we are now, about to become proud parents." He placed his hand on his wife's stomach, watching his hand jump as his child moved underneath it. "I'm really looking forward to it. I don't regret a thing. Even if I've infringed a little on a friendship in the process, it's all worked out perfectly. We'll figure out some way of paying you two back later." He thought a moment. "How about free legal services for the rest of your life?" He looked expectantly to the spot where Greg's head lay resting on Andrea's tummy, noticing the absentminded, loving finger play Greg was being treated to as Andrea's hands roved the thicket of curls, gently massaging the lines of fatigue from the corners of his eyes and teasingly tugging the lobes of his ears.

Karen, too, noticed and musingly commented, "Maybe we've already paid you back, eh Andrea? After all, had we not been living with you, you'd never have met Prince Charming, here."

"Yes, Greg's a very special friend," Andrea responded awkwardly, not exactly sure what else she could say. It certainly wasn't what Greg wanted to hear because she could feel him fall back emotionally—there was a tensing in the mood of the room just before he withdrew physically.

"I'm tired," he announced, stretching and yawning to add veracity to the claim. "Feel free to stay and fire-gaze, guys, but I was up most of the night and need to catch a few winks." He looked at Andrea intently. "I'd hoped you'd be coming with me by this point, light of my life. But I guess we're both relegated to another night of thinking about might-have-beens."

He left the room, but the easy mood was gone. Tim and Karen excused themselves and Andrea went to bed shortly thereafter, but Greg's words continued to buzz through her head—just as he had intended, she was sure.

She lay there a long time. Her foot dangled restlessly out from under the covers. She couldn't sleep. All she could do was think of Greg. The thought of the nights he had mentioned sharing brought a warm flush, and she kicked her foot farther out from under the blankets in a useless attempt to regulate her body temperature.

They'd been in bed a little over an hour. Was that enough of a nap that she could go wake him up for a last little necking session? Sort of a last hurrah, as it were. It just might be possible to work him out of her system once and for all.

She gave the idea serious thought. Maybe if she gave him twenty more minutes. Surely that would be enough sleep to revitalize him.

She listened as a door shut somewhere overhead, followed by the sound of running water. What was wrong up there, for heaven's sake? That was the third trip to the bathroom tonight. She wondered if Greg thought four and five trips to the bathroom every night during a nine-month pregnancy produced a bonding effect in a marriage, or was it just the actual delivery? How did he feel about bonding during the 2:00 a.m. feeding?

Wait a minute, the footsteps were heading in the wrong direction. They were going into the kitchenette, not back to bed. And the lightness of the steps sounded like Karen's. More running water. Andrea could almost visualize the filled teakettle being thumped down on the burner and the flame being flicked on. No other footsteps. Tim must be sleeping.

Andrea wriggled out of the tangle she had created of her blankets. A cup of tea with Karen might be just the thing. Maybe she'd find some herbal so they wouldn't be drinking caffeine at this time of night.

"Hi," she whispered, coming through the door. "You need some company?"

"Hi, yourself," Karen answered back listlessly. "You can't come in. Tim might wake up and come out. He's taken to sleeping in the buff lately. He thinks it's going to save time getting dressed when we have to go to the hospital." Karen shrugged in defeat. "What a joke. I'm going to be pregnant forever."

Andrea pushed the door a little farther open and sidled past Karen's boldly extended stomach. "Don't you worry," she whispered confidentially. "Did I ever tell you about the time Lisa and I decided to get even with Tim after he cut her doll's hair off at the roots and gave it to his hamster to nest with?" She ushered a glum Karen in the direction of the kitchenette. "Let me assure you, what with growing up next door to each other and one thing or another, I've seen pretty much of what that boy has to offer. It would be difficult to offend my tender sensibilities at this point."

Karen laughed in spite of herself. "You guys must have driven your parents wild."

"Oh, we did, we did," Andrea assured her. "Now tell me what your problem is. How come you're still awake?"

"God, I don't know. My back hurts no matter how many back presses I do, the baby's never coming, and I feel so weepy and shaky. I think I'm getting the flu. Even my stomach is all cramped."

Andrea settled back in a kitchen chair and studied the dejected features of her friend's face while they waited for the tea to brew. "Look at it this way: If you catch the flu now, you're sure to be over it by the time you deliver. You've got two and a half weeks left, after all. And I guarantee you, you won't be pregnant forever. The laws of nature preclude the possibility."

Karen gave an unladylike snort, expressing her opinion of the laws of nature. "It'll be just my luck to be the first ten-year pregnancy in the medical books."

"You want me to go downstairs and ask Greg if there's anything you can take to help you sleep?" It was a better reason for waking him up than anything else she had thought of so far.

Her plans were bound for failure, however, as Karen brushed away the offer. "No, don't do that. I'll be fine. Sometimes you just need a good cry, you know?"

Sometimes you needed other things as well. And it was rapidly becoming obvious that Andrea's needs were bound to remain unappeased. Under the circumstances it would be better to be a good scout and try to help Karen since she was the only option available at the moment. "Go get the cards." Andrea sighed in resignation. "We'll play Old Maid and I'll tell you about the time Tim, Lisa and I got assigned the leads in the second-grade production of *Beauty and the Beast*. Lisa was the beauty, Tim was the prince after the beast got kissed, and I was the beast."

Karen was already giggling and Andrea stopped in her narrative to admonish her, "Well, go get the cards. That's not even the funny part. Now that I think about it, breaking the zipper and getting stuck sweating inside a hairy-beast outfit twice my size wasn't particularly funny either."

Peering into the pot sometime later, Karen stopped giggling long enough to inform her cohort, "We're out of tea again. That was the second pot."

"We couldn't be." Andrea leaned forward to inspect the pot and frowned. "I can't believe it. I suppose we'll both float away if we make a third. I was all set to tell you about the sterling blind date that sadist you're married to fixed me up with for the freshman cotillion, too."

Checking the digital clock on the oven, Karen grimaced and announced, "It's three o'clock. We really ought to try to get some sleep. I'm not feeling sorry for myself any more, but my stomach feels worse than ever." She stood up and groaned, "All that tea sloshing around down there. Yuck."

Andrea was drawn toward the living-area window and absently looked out. "No sign of any letup," she advised. "There's darn close to two feet of snow out there." She turned, thinking to tell Karen good-night, and was shocked to find her bent over, gripping a chair back with tightly clenched fists.

"My God, what's wrong? You really are sick, aren't you?"

"It's this damn back. As soon as I think it's letting up, it comes back again. It's going to be one hell of a home stretch if this keeps up."

"I'm going to get Greg," Andrea informed her. "There must be some crazy exercise that could help alleviate that. God knows he had a long enough list of them he wants me to teach." She strode determinedly toward the door leading to the steps. "Don't move. We'll be right back."

Ruthlessly Andrea ripped the pillow Greg clutched from his grasp and shook his shoulder.

"Hmm? What is it?" he groggily responded.

"Wake up, Greg. Karen needs you."

"I'm awake. I'm awake. What does she need?"

"She's been awake all night. Her back's killing her."

"How do you know? Have you been awake too? What's wrong with you?"

Andrea eyed him impatiently. She wasn't going to be drawn into a discussion on that right now. "Never mind why I'm awake. I just am. We've been drinking tea and playing cards but now she's in pain. Listen, would some of those weird things you were describing for that prenatal exercise class you wanted me to teach help her? She needs some sleep."

"Don't we all," Greg observed drolly. He groaned as Andrea ruthlessly pulled the sheet and blanket away. Rolling to the edge of the bed and pulling himself to a sitting position, he sat there for a moment adjusting his eyes to the light before reaching for a robe and gray sweat socks to protect his feet from the chill of the floor. "All right, I'm ready. Lead on. But she had better be in extreme pain."

Evidently Tim had awakened during the interim. His face was twisted into a mask of concern as the two trooped back up the stairs. "Maybe I should call the doctor," he greeted them. "She says she hasn't been to sleep at all yet."

"Oh, for heaven's sake," Greg groaned in despair. "How easily they forget. I am a doctor, an obstetrician even. Remember?"

Andrea laughed at Tim's expression.

"Oh. That's right. You are, aren't you?" Tim stepped back to allow their entrance with a nervous hand raking through his tumbled blond hair and a slightly puzzled look still visible around his eyes. He seemed to be having trouble assimilating the early-morning events. His hand trembled slightly as he gestured them in and there was a slight imploring quality to his tone as he uneasily queried, "Can you see what's wrong, Greg? I'm afraid I'm not much good when someone's sick."

Great, Greg thought, this was just what he needed after last night's delivery. His niece's husband was going to fall apart over a probable muscle spasm. He'd be terrific when delivery time rolled around. But Karen's questioning "Uncle Greg?" caught him up short. Something really was wrong. She hadn't called him Uncle Greg since she had turned fourteen and considered herself all grown up, certainly too mature for uncles only a few years older than herself.

"What's up, sweet pea?" he lightly queried while he studied the white brackets of pain around her mouth and the set, slightly flared nostrils. She stood where Andrea had left her, still gripping the back of the chair with bloodless knuckles. This was more than a back spasm. He'd stake his framed copy of the Hippocratic oath on that.

"First I thought my back was just out of whack. Wouldn't be the first time in the past few months. But now... Oh, Uncle Greg..." She burst into tears. "I'm losing the baby, I just know it. My whole insides are being wrenched out!"

Andrea watched him open his arms to his niece. She noticed Karen's use of Greg's toweling robe to sop up her tears of anguish. She didn't need a doctor to tell her this was serious business. Tim distractedly paced the breadth of the living room, detouring through the small kitchenette area, finally stopping to place both palms on the Formica breakfast table in front of Karen. "You are not losing the baby, Karen. Tell her Greg," he directed. "I'm sure it could be any number of other things."

Oh God. It was all happening again, Andrea thought. Karen was going to lose the baby. Any chance of survival would be ruled out by the freak March blizzard ruthlessly piling and drifting snow outside the tight little bungalow. There was no way to get to a hospital. Even the best doctors needed proper equipment, and the blood-pressure cuff and stethoscope Greg kept at home would only go so far.

How could people open themselves up to this kind of vulnerability? The old it'll-never-happen-to-us syndrome, she supposed. Had there been enough time to build a strong enough relationship between Karen and Tim to weather this kind of strain, or would their marriage fall apart like Peggy and Ted's? Andrea watched from a distance, a detached spectator viewing the unfolding melodrama from the safety of the audience. Her emotions would allow nothing else.

"Come on, baby girl," Greg urged, he too slipping back into childhood terms of endearment. "We're not giving up that easily. It's too late for you to lose the baby. Even if we deliver it within the next ten minutes, chances are it'll be fine. It's only a few weeks early, not months and months, and your calculations could have been off by that much, you know. Not to worry. Here, put your arms up around my neck and stick your backside out a bit."

As she followed his directions, Greg put his palms low on her back, just above the swell of her buttocks. Andrea could see the sinewy muscles in his arms contract and harden as he used his weight to apply pressure to the area. "Feel better, honey?"

"No," Karen whimpered. "That makes my back feel better, but now I'm nauseated and trembly. There's something wrong, I know it."

Greg looked to Andrea over Karen's head. "Pull out the kitchen chair," he directed her. "Come on, honey. Sit here." He backed her up until the backs of her knees were against the chair. "Put your arms on the table and rest your head on them. That's it." He glanced up. "Tim, you lean over the back of the chair, put your hands here and press. Got it?"

Tim nodded in a distracted manner, clearly still worried, although Greg's professional manner had gone a long way to reducing the panicky tension in the room.

"Now it's my professional judgment that while you two insomniacs were up here sloshing in the tea, Karen was in preliminary labor. By all the signs, she's well into transition now."

Tim looked up. His befuddled mind homed in on the only pertinent point he had been able to grasp. "You mean she's in labor? The baby's coming? Oh, my God," he groaned as Greg nodded in affirmation. "What are we going to do?"

"We are going to remain calm," Greg directed with a meaningful glare over Karen's head. "There's no way of knowing how long this stage of labor will last. If the snow lets up anytime soon and the plows get out, she may very well still deliver in the safety of a hospital bed. If not, remember that lots of women choose a home delivery. It's not the end of the world."

Two hours flew by under Greg's determined orchestration. "Andrea, see if you can make it next door to borrow some disposable diapers. I hope Jimmy's kid brother isn't toilet trained yet. We'll need them later."

He paused to thoughtfully consider a few more necessities. "Tim, find the heating pad. We can use it to keep the cradle warm until we're sure the baby's temperature has stabilized. Oh, and while you're downstairs, get one of my stretchiest sweat socks, preferably one with a hole so we don't waste a good one. We'll cut off the foot, tie off the stretchy top and use it for a hat on the baby to conserve body heat. All the newborns at Evanston Hospital get little stretch caps. We can do just as well. I'm going to do a quick examination while you're gone. Come on, sweet pea, I'll help you over to the bed."

"Oh, Andrea, you back already?"

Breathlessly, Andrea thrust a handful of toddler-size diapers at him. "She's got more if we need 'em," she gasped. "Oh...and she sent this bulb thing. Some kind of nasal syringe they gave her at the hospital. She said they used it during Rex's birth, but she's never needed it since and Karen's welcome to it."

Greg looked at the small blue plastic aspirator as though someone had just handed him the Hope diamond. There was a touch of awe in his voice as he breathed, "That's wonderful. A real help. This baby will be born with all the amenities."

"Also, here's four receiving blankets. They've been washed in baby detergent."

His spirit clearly renewed, Greg rubbed his hands together and declared, "Now we're cooking. We need your sewing shears and a way to sterilize a few things. Have we got any rubbing alcohol? Where'd you put that brush you use for scrubbing under fingernails? I want to be sure my hands are as clean as we can get them..."

Minutes later, Greg was back. He and Tim had Karen propped up in the bed in a semiupright position. "Okay, baby girl, prop your legs up and let them fall apart. I think we're closing in on the end of this little ordeal, you'll be glad to hear. Let's just check."

The only sound during his brief examination was from a snowplow on the main street a few blocks away. It was too late to do them much good.

Before Greg even said anything, Andrea knew from his expression that this was it. His words only confirmed it. "Okay, kids, it's time to go to work. The main event is all set to go." Andrea only wished she was. She watched in speechless fascination as Greg calmly directed the scenario. "Sit all the way up, Karen, and hold your knees. That's it. Tim, get on the bed behind her and help support her. Great."

Greg laid his large hand on Karen's stomach to feel the start of her next contraction. "Here we go. Deep cleansing breath, Karen, and release it. Deep breath again, hold and push as long as you can." Karen's breath wooshed out and Greg looked up. "Don't waste the contraction, honey, grab another breath and keep pushing. You can make up for it between pains...."

Twenty minutes later, everyone in the room was covered with a fine sheen of perspiration. Especially Karen. The delivery was going to be tough.

Greg had made Karen move to the end of the bed, and he leaned over her there, trying to widen the birth canal. He spoke without even looking up. "I'll tell you one thing, this is no preemie. This little stinker's bigger than some of my full-term babies."

Within a few minutes the baby's head had emerged completely and Andrea was surprised when Greg stopped there. She looked anxiously from Greg to the soon-to-be newborn's head and back to Greg. The baby wasn't crying. Didn't they all cry right away? What was normal? Greg reached for the blue plastic aspirator and directed, "Pant, Karen. Don't push. I know it's hard. The urge is overwhelming, but try hard. Tim, pant with her. Short and shallow. That's it." He wielded the aspirator with efficient, economical moves and managed to clear the infant's air passages; there was a collective sigh when the baby gave a short, faint whimper.

"Now," Greg breathed in relief, "let's get the little devil out into the light and see what we've got here... go ahead, honey, push for all you're worth."

As Greg eased his grand-nephew into the world, and Karen's labors were coming to an end there was the sound of the snowplow turning down their block. By the time Karen had the baby on her tummy Andrea had called the paramedics.

Minutes dragged by but the ambulance finally arrived. After struggling with their litter up the unshoveled walk the paramedics carried Karen and the baby down the two flights of stairs. Thank goodness the blizzard had lessened to a few stubborn flakes. Greg squeezed into the back of the ambulance with Tim as he continued to monitor Karen's condition. There was no room for Andrea. She had to stay behind by herself, unable to follow as her car was thoroughly blocked in the garage by the snow-clogged alley. She watched with wide eyes set in a white face as the paramedics prepared to close the rear ambulance doors.

Greg happened to glance up and see her shaken mien. "Don't worry," he called as one door was locked into place. "We'll take care of her. Once I get her to the hospital, I guarantee she'll be okay." He smiled that special endearing grin of his, but the paramedic closed the other door on it, severing her from its warmth.

Andrea watched the ambulance pull away. Through its rear window she could see Tim clutching the swaddled baby. Then the ambulance turned onto Central Street and out of her sight. For a long time she just stood there, thinking. There was a missing piece here. She could feel it, just out of conscious reach. She gave up as she realized she was shivering. She went inside and put the teakettle on again. At this rate she was going to run out of teabags before she could get to the store for replacements.

Busy. She needed to keep busy. She absently beat the floor with a sock-clad foot. Working at stripping the Murphy bed was totally unappealing. So was cleaning out her linen closet. There was no book or magazine that looked interesting in the entire two flats. Finally she got down a one-thousand-piece jigsaw puzzle of a huge plate of spaghetti and spent three hours separating edge pieces from middles and trying to fit them together.

Then, when she thought she could stand it no longer, Greg was back. He'd taken a taxi from the hospital, and he looked bushed as he shucked his down coat and curved cold hands around the mug of hot tea Andrea held out to him. It was only natural to discuss the early morning's events.

"So that's the awe-inspiring, bonding process of giving birth," Andrea said.

"It wasn't a very good example."

"It certainly isn't a neat process, is it?"

"You have to remember that this was *not* a normal delivery. You're never going to want to get married and have a baby after seeing that, are you? I guess I don't blame you," Greg disclaimed disgustedly. "It was pretty bad." He left the counter he had been leaning against and started walking to his bedroom, believing for the first time he really was going to lose their little war.

Surprisingly, Andrea returned, "You were wonderful. So calm and in control." She barely heard his response as she was stopped in her tracks by a blinding realization.

Calm and in control. *Calm and in control!* And there it was, as clear and definite as the March wind off Lake Michigan. It was the missing piece. This had not been an easy birth. He'd said so himself. Things had gone wrong. The baby had been too big for Karen and even had breathing problems. There had been real danger. Yet Greg had been the epitome of cool, doing what needed doing and never losing his professionalism. And that had been with his own niece, someone she knew he loved. She thought of her own light bout with the flu and contrasted his behavior then.

HOUSE CALLS

Greg had absolutely fallen apart. She hadn't realized the significance of that then, but... he had to love her! He had to love Andrea herself, not merely the image of a wife and generic home life a wife would provide. She held on to his bedroom doorframe, looking at him through new eyes. Suddenly, she knew—she was as certain of his love as she could ever be.

"You say it's not always like that?"

"I said it, but I can't guarantee it. Rough deliveries do happen." Greg threw himself backward on his bed and laid the back of his arm over his eyes and forehead. Andrea sat cross-legged at the bottom of the bed, studying his drawn, tired features with compassion.

"I can see how that kind of thing can really take it out of you. You must have been terrified of losing Karen. What would you do it if had been me? Would you have been so calm?"

"I doubt we'll ever find out after this disaster," Greg grunted in disgust.

Andrea pulled at the blanket as she said, "Oh, I don't know about that."

Quickly Greg raised his head up off the mattress, his narrowed eyes almost pinning her to the bed. "What are you saying?"

Andrea shrugged. "Maybe all the pain and fuss is a way of ensuring we stop and note the specialness of the event."

"You mean that?" he questioned uncertainly, hope beginning to flare in his mahogany eyes.

Andrea looked him directly in the eye for the first time in several weeks. "Greg, have you completely given up on me? Is it possible for you to still love me after the hard time I've given you?"

He answered impatiently. "I told you over and over again that I loved you. For some reason you have refused to accept it."

Her eyes didn't waver from his. "I'm asking you here and now. Do you love me, now... today?"

"Yes," he answered unequivocally. "I do."

She sat back on her heels. "I love you, too."

Cautiously, he continued. "And you'll marry me?"

"Absolutely."

"When?"

She put her finger to her mouth, thinking. "Mmm, if you weren't so exhausted, I would suggest we look for someplace within walking distance that could do a blood test. That's how sure I am. I accept that you love me. Do you accept my love in return?"

He collapsed back on the bed in sheer relief. "I've known all along you loved me. The problem has been getting you to admit it." He let out a stream of air. "Thank God. I thought for a while there I'd have to actually find an apartment by this weekend. I was never so glad to see a late-winter blizzard in my life."

"What?" she shrieked, not believing her ears.

"I was trying to push you into a decision, my love. I never thought you'd let me leave when I gave my ultimatum. But you were going to let me go, weren't you? Lord, I was scared." He raised his head to look at her. "What made you change your mind?"

She looked discomfited. "Actually, it was the difference in the way you handled my little headache and Karen's major problems. The light dawned about ten minutes ago."

"Well, I'll be." He thought about that for a minute and cleared his throat, collecting himself. "Well, I hope nearly losing one relative was enough to convince you for a good long time because I'm not sure I could go through another ordeal like that one to prove myself again." He was quiet for a moment before gathering himself again. "But be that as it may, let's discuss my fatigue for a moment. Maybe if you made a little lunch while I took a shower, I could revive myself enough for a hike to the clinic. It's only a mile or so. What do you say?"

"The quickest would be creamed tuna on toast," Andrea warned.

"You going to make it with cream of mushroom soup?"

"I could check if they have any cream of celery next door, but it'll take longer."

"Never mind. I'll close my eyes and offer it up in the interests of getting this little project under way before you have time to change your mind. Uh... Now, about christening our firstborn, Emmett—"

"Oh, good heavens! Don't press your luck. I said that I loved you, not that I'd gone over the brink into insanity. I'll make a deal: I'll make the lunch, we'll eat it, get the tests and license, and you can work on converting me."

And he did, directly afterward.

* * * * *

A breathtaking roller coaster of adventure, passion and danger in the dazzling Roaring Twenties!

SCANDALOUS SPIRITS

ERIN YORKE

Running from unspeakable danger, she found shelter—and desire—in the arms of a reckless stranger.

Available in January at your favorite retail outlet, or reserve your copy for December shipping by sending your name, address, zip or postal code along with a check or money order for $5.25 (include 75¢ for postage and handling) payable to Worldwide Library to:

In the U.S.	In Canada
Worldwide Library	Worldwide Library
901 Fuhrmann Blvd.	P.O. Box 609
Box 1325	Fort Erie, Ontario
Buffalo, NY 14269-1325	L2A 5X3

Please specify book title with your order.

WORLDWIDE LIBRARY

SCA-1

Take 4 Silhouette Intimate Moments novels and a surprise gift
FREE

Then preview 4 brand-new Silhouette Intimate Moments novels—delivered to your door as soon as they come off the presses! If you decide to keep them, you pay just $2.49 each*—a 9% saving off the retail price, *with no additional charges for postage and handling!*

Silhouette Intimate Moments novels are not for everyone. They were created to give you a more detailed, more exciting reading experience, filled with romantic fantasy, intense sensuality and stirring passion.

Start with 4 Silhouette Intimate Moments novels and a surprise gift absolutely FREE. They're yours to keep without obligation. You can always return a shipment and cancel at any time.

Simply fill out and return the coupon today!

* Plus 49¢ postage and handling per shipment in Canada.

Silhouette Intimate Moments®

Clip and mail to: Silhouette Books

In U.S.:
901 Fuhrmann Blvd.
P.O. Box 9013
Buffalo, NY 14240-9013

In Canada:
P.O. Box 609
Fort Erie, Ontario
L2A 5X3

YES! Please rush me 4 free Silhouette Intimate Moments novels and my free surprise gift. Then send me 4 Silhouette Intimate Moments novels to preview each month as soon as they come off the presses. Bill me at the low price of $2.49 each*—a 9% saving off the retail price. There is no minimum number of books I must purchase. I can always return a shipment and cancel at any time. Even if I never buy another book from Silhouette Intimate Moments, the 4 free novels and surprise gift are mine to keep forever.

* Plus 49¢ postage and handling per shipment in Canada.

240 BPO BP7F

Name _____ (please print) _____

Address _____ Apt. _____

City _____ State/Prov. _____ Zip/Postal Code _____

This offer is limited to one order per household and not valid to present subscribers. Price is subject to change.

IM-SUB-1D

ATTRACTIVE, SPACE SAVING BOOK RACK

Display your most prized novels on this handsome and sturdy book rack. The hand-rubbed walnut finish will blend into your library decor with quiet elegance, providing a practical organizer for your favorite hard-or soft-covered books.

Only $9.95

Approximately 16" x 8" when assembled

Assembles in seconds!

To order, rush your name, address and zip code, along with a check or money order for $10.70* ($9.95 plus 75¢ postage and handling) payable to *Silhouette Books*.

Silhouette Books
Book Rack Offer
901 Fuhrmann Blvd.
P.O. Box 1396
Buffalo, NY 14269-1396

Offer not available in Canada.

*New York and Iowa residents add appropriate sales tax.

Silhouette Romance

COMING NEXT MONTH

#556 NEVER LOVE A COWBOY—Rita Rainville
Anne Sheldon thought she was resigned to widowhood and could live off her happy memories, but Ben Benedict knew better. He was sure Anne deserved a future as well as a past—a future that included him.

#557 DONOVAN'S MERMAID—Helen R. Myers
Chief of police Sam Donovan was Gulls Drift's most confirmed bachelor until he rescued Miranda Paley from the Gulf of Mexico. Now Sam's heart needed rescuing from Randi's captivating smile. Would the little town of Gulls Drift ever be the same?

#558 A KISS IS STILL A KISS—Colleen Christie
Kurt Lawrence needed feisty Margo Shepherd to help him revamp his video chain. But after an impulsive kiss and a case of mistaken identity, how could he assure her he was strictly business? Especially when the memory of her lips had him longing to mix business with pleasure....

#559 UNDER A DESERT SKY—Arlene James
Jamie Goff had been born in the Nevada desert, and her heart had always belonged under an endless sky. But when citified Bronson Taylor laid claim to her love, Jamie was torn—Bron must return to the city. Would Jamie have to choose between her two loves?

#560 THE OUTSIDER—Stella Bagwell
Luke Chandler had arrived just in the nick of time to save Faith Galloway's ranch, but Faith felt more than gratitude for her mysterious new employee. Was Faith's love strong enough to convince the handsome drifter that it was time to settle down?

#561 WIFE WANTED—Terri Herrington
Tycoon Joe Dillon had launched the perfect advertising campaign to find himself a wife, but the woman he wanted hadn't applied for the job. He'd have to do some powerful persuading to show "happily single" Brit Alexander that the man behind the slogans had a heart of gold....

AVAILABLE THIS MONTH:

#550 A MATTER OF HONOR
Brittany Young

#551 THE BEWITCHING HOUR
Jennifer Mikels

#552 HOUSE CALLS
Terry Essig

#553 SEASON OF THE HEART
Pat Warren

#554 AUTHOR'S CHOICE
Elizabeth August

#555 CINDY AND THE PRINCE
Debbie Macomber

Silhouette Romance™
Legendary Lovers Trilogy

BY DEBBIE MACOMBER....

ONCE UPON A TIME, in a land not so far away, there lived a girl, Debbie Macomber, who grew up dreaming of castles, white knights and princes on fiery steeds. Her family was an ordinary one with a mother and father and one wicked brother, who sold copies of her diary to all the boys in her junior high class.

One day, when Debbie was only nineteen, a handsome electrician drove by in a shiny black convertible. Now Debbie knew a prince when she saw one, and before long they lived in a two-bedroom cottage surrounded by a white picket fence.

As often happens when a damsel fair meets her prince charming, children followed, and soon the two-bedroom cottage became a four-bedroom castle. The kingdom flourished and prospered, and between soccer games and car pools, ballet classes and clarinet lessons, Debbie thought about love and enchantment and the magic of romance.

One day Debbie said, "What this country needs is a good fairy tale." She remembered how well her diary had sold and she dreamed again of castles, white knights and princes on fiery steeds. And so the stories of Cinderella, Beauty and the Beast, and Snow White were reborn....

Look for Debbie Macomber's *Legendary Lovers* trilogy from Silhouette Romance: *Cindy and the Prince* (January, 1988); *Some Kind of Wonderful* (March, 1988); *Almost Paradise* (May, 1988). Don't miss them!